LAND
RUSH

Also by Gary Reiswig

Water Boy, a novel

*The Thousand Mile Stare: One Family's Journey
Through the Struggle & Science of Alzheimer's*

LAND
RUSH

Stories from the Great Plains

GARY REISWIG

Archway Publishing books may be ordered through booksellers or by contacting:

Archway Publishing
1663 Liberty Drive
Bloomington, IN 47403
www.archwaypublishing.com
1-(888)-242-5904

Because of the dynamic nature of the Internet, any web addresses or links contained in this book may have changed since publication and may no longer be valid. The views expressed in this work are solely those of the author and do not necessarily reflect the views of the publisher, and the publisher hereby disclaims any responsibility for them.

Certain stock imagery © Thinkstock.
Any people depicted in stock imagery provided by Thinkstock are models, and such images are being used for illustrative purposes only.

Interior images by Annemarie McCoy

ISBN: 978-1-4808-0920-8 (e)
ISBN: 978-1-4808-0919-2 (sc)

Library of Congress Control Number: 2014944896

Printed in the United States of America

Archway Publishing rev. date: 7/29/2014

In memory of

My parents,
John Fred and Della May

My sister and brother,
Lela Jane and David Earl

My grandparents,
John and Molly Reiswig
Arthur and Alda Gregory

CONTENTS

PREFACE

THESE STORIES ARE BASED ON TRUE EVENTS.

To avoid frightening anyone and offending the National Park Service, I make the following disclaimer: to my knowledge, no mule has ever fallen off the Bright Angel Trail. The story "Bright Angel Trail" is based on true events to the extent that I have conveyed the awe and terror I experienced when I visited the Grand Canyon myself. The canyon was glorious, awesome, overwhelming and terrifying, heaven and hell both expressed so well by nature's handiwork.

The cultural importance of high school football in Oklahoma is as I have expressed it in "Fair Game." I played quarterback in high school, but did so without the skills of Danny. I'm sure I would have been a star water boy. I have conveyed the truth about war and the love and admiration of an uncle in "Two Door Hardtop." There was a box supper, and we had a neighbor like Dootie Poor who pulled the snake trick on my mother.

Elements within the story "Fair Game" appeared in my novel *Water Boy*.

In a different form, elements from the first and last stories, "The Buffalo Roam: And, Then, What Next?" and the essay "Free Land" appeared in my memoir, *The Thousand Mile Stare*. They are memoir while the other stories are fiction.

Photo by the Herald Democrat taken in the 1950's

Siblings at the Egbert House

Honeymoon

First Bareback Ride

Ready to Ride Pioneer Parade

Buffalo Trails

Twins

Before She Disappeared

THE BUFFALO ROAM:
AND, THEN, WHAT NEXT?

"Don't bother with the tractor. Let's work the calves today," Dad said when we finished the morning chores. I was twelve, about to enter seventh grade, and had been working in the field for two or three years, long enough that driving the tractor had lost its novelty.

"You don't like plowing that field much anyhow, do you?" he added.

A stab of regret and guilt sliced into me. I looked down at my boots. They were caked with manure, so I cleaned them on the foot scraper Dad had forged in the shop. It was expertly crafted and could have passed for a manufactured item. Mother insisted it be placed on the steps coming up from the barn to minimize the amount of barnyard dirt we carried to the house. Dad made it look decorative and professional to please her.

There was a reason I didn't enjoy plowing the field northwest of the house. Next to the field lay a wide patch of grass where the terraces drained. In the grass, scavengers had scattered the remains of our dog, matted tufts of hair attached to dried skin and bleached bones. In death, her jaw and teeth appeared to be locked in a snarl, although she had been a sweetheart and had never bitten anyone or even growled at one of the family.

My sister and I had begged Mom and Dad for a collie. We wanted to name her Lassie after the collie in a series of books we had read. She arrived on the train in a small crate from a breeder in Iowa. Although she was our dog, I was the one who took care of her and made sure she was fed so she, unlike other farm dogs, wouldn't feel tempted to kill chickens. I also supplied fresh water so she wasn't forced to drink from the pond or the stock tank when she was thirsty.

To me she was a near-perfect example of the collie breed, although she was part shepherd. She had the white and yellow hair of a full-blooded collie, a long nose, and dark, inquisitive eyes. She died after a series of events that began on a Sunday as we were getting ready to leave for church. A stranger drove into the farmyard, and Dad answered when the man knocked on the door.

"You have a beautiful collie." That was the first thing the man said. I had followed Dad to see what the stranger wanted.

I slid in front of Dad to explain. "She's part shepherd. She's a good herder. My dad knew she would be." The fact that she wasn't a purebred had bothered me when my parents purchased her, but after her arrival, I was won over by her collie looks and her personality. She was good with the cattle even when she was still a puppy, so I came to understand that being a mixed breed was an asset, just as Dad had insisted it was when my parents ordered her. I thought they were only saving money because she cost half as much as a purebred. But Dad claimed he knew the shepherd blood was important, that it would make her a good worker. That's why he'd insisted on the mix. I was proud of what Dad had accomplished with our farm. I wanted the man to know how smart he was.

The stranger told Dad he wanted to look at the irrigation system. Dad explained that the family was on its way to church. The man was welcome to look around, but if he wanted to talk about what he saw, he'd have to come back another time. "We never miss church and Sunday school," Dad explained. "The kids have perfect attendance."

The request for information about irrigation wasn't unusual because my father was the first farmer in Beaver County, Oklahoma, to install an irrigation system with sprinkler pipe supplied with water pumped from a well. People were curious. What does irrigated sorghum look like compared to the dry land crop? How much work is it to move the pipe? How can a man tell if there's enough water under his land for irrigation?

Phone service hadn't started in the part of the county where we lived, so people just showed up at a time that was convenient for them. The man who had arrived that Sunday certainly had little interest in church, or he wouldn't have chosen that day for a tour. I thought later that should have been a warning to us that there might be trouble, and I wished I hadn't touted the collie to be such a good dog. When we returned from church that afternoon, she was gone.

I felt in my heart the stranger had stolen her and that I was mostly responsible. My parents thought she'd left of her own accord and would return. This was not the first time a dog of ours had disappeared. A few years earlier, a crossbreed male—Irish setter and spaniel—showed up at the farm, stayed long enough for us kids to adopt him as our own and name him Rex, and then he left. Not unusual behavior for an unneutered male dog, our parents explained. I didn't fully understand then the relevance of being unneutered, but I was older when the collie disappeared. I understood breeding and genetics, how the collie would never be a breeding animal because she was a mixed-blood and had been spayed. I also knew she was well cared for and had no reason to leave the farm. I felt she loved me as much as I loved her. I didn't think she had left of her own accord. I wanted Dad to contact the sheriff, who sometimes attended our church. The sheriff had a dog, and I thought he would be sympathetic.

"Tell him about the man who came to the house on Sunday," I insisted.

"I don't know the man or where he's from. I think he said he was from out around Hooker, another county. Our sheriff has no jurisdiction there."

"Then contact the sheriff of that county," I argued.

"What shall I say?" Dad asked. "One of your citizens might have been at my farm, and maybe he stole my dog?"

I had read all the Hardy Boys detective novels. I thought I knew a little something about investigating crimes. "Give the sheriff a description of the man's pickup, and ask him if he knows anyone who drives that kind of truck. Tell him it's someone who's thinking about putting in an irrigation system and someone who doesn't go to church. Ask if he's seen anyone riding around with a collie dog, because a man was on our farm, maybe from your county, the same day our dog went missing." Tears of grief ran down my face by the time I had spilled all those words.

"I don't even know what kind of pickup he drove," Dad admitted. "Do you remember?"

I thought it might have been a Chevy, three or four years old, but I wasn't sure. A neutral color, green, or gray, or—I had no idea. Frank and Joe Hardy would have been more observant. I was upset and blamed myself more and more for the collie's disappearance.

My mother and I drove all directions from the farm, asking neighbors if they had seen her, but no one had. She had disappeared without a trace.

I had been grieving for a month when the collie showed up at the one-room school my younger brother and I attended. She was gaunt, afraid of everyone, wouldn't let anyone touch her except me. Her coat was dirty and tangled with cockleburs. She looked like a woman who had gone out of the house with her hair in rollers and got caught in a ferocious windstorm. She had sores on her feet as if she'd traveled a great distance.

When my mother picked us up at school, the dog refused to get in the car, kneeling down on her belly with her face between her paws, whining and trembling.

"Someone definitely stole her," Mother admitted. "She must have escaped. Maybe she was headed home, came near the school, and picked up your scent. If only she could talk."

I was happy to have her back, but I was in a rage over the extent of her suffering and because I had endured so much grief myself. The dog lay around, ate and drank little, and slept most of the day. She looked even more pitiful after Mother used scissors to cut out the burs. At night, the collie stayed awake, pacing back and forth.

Before she disappeared, milking time was the highlight of her day. To bring in the cows, I rode the horse and she followed me, easing any wanderers back on the path to the barn. After her return, she wasn't interested in helping. She stayed close to the house seeking shade.

The veterinarian could identify nothing specific wrong with her, but her spirit never returned. To my dad she was useless if she was not interested in helping with the work. He insisted she had to be put down. He asked me to shoot her.

It wasn't that Dad wanted to shirk the job. Rather, he wanted to cultivate my ability to discharge that kind of difficult but necessary responsibility. He had asked me to shoot a steer we had been fattening for the spring butchering time. I had done it and felt good about accomplishing the task. I believed myself to be an excellent shot, confident I could put the animal down with the minimum amount of pain inflicted. But I wasn't able to bring myself to shoot the collie.

I didn't even know where Dad had shot her until I discovered her remains while I plowed. After seeing the collie's bones, I reviewed the whole string of events leading up to her death: how Dad had been overly trusting and failed to obtain the identity of the stranger when he appeared that Sunday, how I had almost encouraged the man to steal her by bragging, how I had failed to initiate a satisfactory investigation. Then I let Dad shoot her. That was my biggest failure. If I was unable to persuade him to spare her life, I should have been the one to take her life. I would still have felt the guilt and sadness, but I thought she would have understood the desperation of her situation had it been me with the gun, and she would have known how hard it was for me to shoot her. At least that's the script that played itself in my mind. I also would have taken the time to bury her out of my love and respect. Because I had not faced my responsibility, it was difficult to look at her bones when I circled the field.

This sadness about the dog was on my mind as I finished scraping my boots. My dad said, "Before you go up to the house for breakfast, catch the horses. I'll throw out a couple of hay bales and put some cake in the troughs, then call the cows. Maybe they'll come on their own and save us a long ride."

I found the feed bucket, caught the two bay horses, and let them loose in the corral. The bays were full brother and sister. They had replaced our pinto, Skyrocket, after he had, Houdini-like, opened the barn door and the lid to the feed bin, where he ate all he wanted of the grain mixture we fed to the milk cows. It was not a severe case of foundering, or laminitis, but it was bad enough to keep him from being a good cow horse, which sometimes demands running full speed and sharp turns. Skyrocket could not make those moves on sore feet, the main symptom of being foundered.

A man who lived a few miles west and who knew my dad when they were young had seen my sister and me ride Skyrocket Indian style in the Pioneer Days Parade. The man said he wanted the horse for his little girl to ride and asked Dad if he'd sell the pinto. After the horse foundered himself and would never chase another wild cow, Dad offered to sell him. Of course, he explained why. Dad never did anything shady. Sometimes we drove by their place and saw Skyrocket in the pasture. He was heavier. That can happen after foundering if the horse doesn't get enough exercise. We kids thought Skyrocket missed us. My parents assured us he was having a good life, taking it easy, and letting one little girl ride him. My sister and I tried to look at the situation in that positive light. Still, we considered Skyrocket to be our horse, like Lassie was our dog.

The lost, loved animals were on my mind as I neared the house and heard Dad sing his shrill, yodeling cattle call. I was proud I could do a cattle call as well as—if not better than—he could. I hoped the cattle wouldn't come. I wanted to ride. It might help me get out of my dark mood, although my dad would insist I mount up on Dusty, the gelding, because he always rode Lady, a filly with a gait so smooth it felt like riding a rocking chair. She was high-spirited with long fine bones and a bright-eyed Arabian head. By keeping records on the registered Hereford cattle we owned, I had learned a great deal about how fickle genetics can be. The same bull and cow or sire and dam can produce offspring of very different conformation and quality year to year. Dusty, Lady's older brother by a year, felt nothing like a rocking chair. He rode more like a pack mule.

My dad came in for breakfast. "The cattle are probably in the southeast corner. There's some wind. I doubt they heard me. Lady still needs some training anyhow." Dad had recently sold the filly. The new owner, from Wichita, Kansas, had paid a handsome price, and he was due to pick her up in a month. We'd soon be left with one horse—her jug-headed, rough-gaited brother. I tried to ignore the grief I was already stifling.

Mother hummed one of the show tunes she'd learned off the radio while she filled our plates with bacon and eggs. Dad and I ate, walked back to the corral, and saddled the horses. Dusty had a habit of extending his girth, then relaxing once his rider mounted. You had to give the gelding credit—he was smart. That was the one thing Dusty had in common with our former horse, Skyrocket.

Both of them could open the latch of any gate, unless the latch was tied down with baling wire. I took my time, tightening the cinch several times, the only way to outwit him. I also wanted to delay the lesson I knew was coming, another one of those difficult but necessary farm lessons, like killing the steer at butchering time, or shooting the dog after she no longer was inclined to work.

When we topped the low rise east of the house, we could see the cattle still nearly a mile away, forty or fifty cows, with calves that had been born in the early spring. The calves had to be vaccinated and dehorned, and the young bulls castrated. We reined the horses to a stop, and Dad called again. "Aaaaaaa-weeeeeeeeee-oooooooooooo!" Some of the cows lifted their heads. They had heard, but they didn't move.

"Grass has been too good. We'll have to drive them every step of the way," Dad muttered. We kicked the horses into a lope. When we got closer, we slowed down to keep the cows from scattering. Most of them quit grazing and watched us. Some of the cows made low moaning sounds almost like a croon to call their calves. Dad pulled Lady to a stop.

"Look. Ever notice this?" He pointed to a knoll in front of us. When he wanted to teach me a lesson, my dad used a special elevated tone that wasn't natural for him. Sometimes I appreciated his attempts to help me understand things and sometimes not. I knew when he taught me in that tone of voice he, at the same time, expected something back from me, something vague but important, I suspected. I looked in the direction he pointed, but I didn't see anything unusual.

"Notice what?"

"See the cattle trail? Look again. To the right and to the left."

There were a number of undulations a few feet apart running parallel with the cattle trail until they ended at a washout. Now that I saw them, they looked like old trails the grass had grown over.

"Buffalo trails. Buffalo made trails just like cattle. Thousands of them, millions maybe, walking single file, side by side. Likely the herd came by this precise spot only once but still made those deep trails because there were so many animals following one after the other. I read about it in the *Farmer Stockman*. There's trails all over the panhandle."

"But those other ones disappear. The cattle trail goes on."

"Dust Bowl filled the trails with dirt in most places. When it rained again, the grass grew back over, and they were gone. But if you follow the line of these trails and ride north or south, you'll see remnants of them as far the grass grows."

I could see two miles or more to the south. A quarter-mile ahead, across the highway, the low roof of my Uncle Harvey's dugout glinted in the sun along with the rounded Quonset barn. Harvey was just younger than my dad in the string of fourteen siblings. He had chiseled their house into a south-facing bluff, building what would be the basement of the house they ultimately planned to build. That day had not yet arrived. Still, the dugout was warm in the winter and cool in the summer because it was a dugout just like many of the first homes had been in pioneer days. They could walk out of their front door at ground level because the sides of the house were built into the prairie hillside. They had little concern about tornadoes, and there was no need for a separate storm cellar. Beyond their place, I could see more of the grass-covered undulations on a stretch of their pasture.

As I scanned the terrain, I cataloged the signs of civilization: barbed wire fences, a state road that had been blacktopped, the poles with power lines that carried public electricity, which had recently arrived in this part of the panhandle, and the radio tower of the Northern Natural Gas plant with its red light. Even with all that modern imposition, it was easy to imagine the bison shambling across the prairie, following each other for miles and miles. A low-riding dust cloud hovered over the herd as their hooves gouged the trails that were a foot deep.[1]

I looked toward an escarpment, a chalky ravine with sandstone layers, where a few years earlier my sister and I had carved our initials into a layer of the sandstone. Near the stone, we had found chipped red flint that we took home and kept in box. A band of Native Americans had once been there making arrowheads probably waiting on buffalo to pass by, maybe the very herd that had made the trails.

A year or two later, my sister developed breasts and refused to play our old childish games about outlaws and lawmen, but I once persuaded her to return to the canyon to see if our initials were still on the rock. After we found them, we noticed a flat cave about three feet wide and a foot high beneath a layer of rock higher up on the side of the ravine. We climbed the clay bank to look at it. Once our eyes adjusted to the darkness in the cave, we discovered a den of rattlesnakes near the end of their hibernation sliding over each other like tangled ropes. More scared than we had been one time when lightning struck the ground less than a hundred feet from where we played, we scampered and slid down the loose slope, hit the canyon floor, and dashed toward home. As we ran, I checked my pocket to make sure my knife was there in case we were bitten. Who knew how many rattlers were between us and the house? We had been taught to slice through the fang marks and make the bite bleed. Could I do that? Cut an x, suck out the poisoned blood, and spit it on the ground. That was the surest

---

1   The great migrating herds of bison had been split in two by the transcontinental railroads beginning around 1870. The northern herd grazed north of Nebraska, and the southern herd grazed south of Kansas. Eventually, the southern herd was squeezed into the Oklahoma Panhandle. The last old bull of the southern herd was killed in 1890 not far west of where my dad and I were rounding up cattle. Bison could have disappeared like the passenger pigeon, the last of which died in captivity in 1920. The buffalo story turned out better. When the Wichita Mountain Preserve was established in western Oklahoma in 1906, the first animals for its buffalo herd were purchased from the Bronx Zoo in New York City. After that, with the help of visionary preservationists, large herds of bison, private and public, have come back and still roam.

way to prevent death from snakebite. Or so we'd once been told by our teacher at Garrett School.

Remembering the snakes, I shivered as my dad gave me the lesson about the buffalo trails. I was glad the stone slabs with the carved initials and the cave, if they still existed, were a quarter mile away from where I sat astride Dusty. For the moment, I was safe.

Dad lifted his fist and shouted, "Let's drive them calves home." The cows all stopped grazing. We had their attention. Dad reined Lady to the left, and I wheeled Dusty to the right. We eased our way behind the cattle. The animals headed toward the barn walking single file on the trail first cut by the buffalo. I missed the collie. She had always hazed the stragglers.

Once the cows were pointed in the direction of the barn, we counted to make sure none of the herd was missing. We both rode the flanks near the end of the line to prevent any wary cow-calf pairs from bolting. Only an hour after we finished breakfast, we had the animals penned inside the corral. Most of the cows ate the hay and cake Dad had put out for them, ignoring everything else. The more nervous ones, the better mothers, kept track of their calves even while they grabbed a bite of alfalfa. We tied the horses to the fence half the length of a football field away from where we planned to work.

Dad hadn't given me instructions, so I did what I'd done before: loosened the lariat on Dusty's saddle and caught the first calf, a heifer, and held her down while Dad gave her an injection and dehorned her. I caught a second calf, another heifer, and dragged her over to where my dad had set up the equipment and medicine. He grinned at me. "Looks like we're doing all the heifers first."

I had known from the moment my dad announced we'd be working the calves that this was the day of a lesson I had avoided as long as I could. The treatise about the buffalo trails was an educational bonus. The curriculum for the day called for the lesson all farm boys faced sooner or later: how to castrate a young bull.

Farm boys know well the results of castration, how much easier it is to handle a steer than a bull, a gelding compared to a stallion, a shoat instead of a boar. Bulls are aggressive, dominant, and proud. They're combative if challenged and will break down fences to reach a heifer in heat. Steers are non-assertive and easily controlled. The castration of a young bull is so simple, it was expected that a twelve-year-old boy should be able to perform the surgery.

With the next loop, I caught a sturdy young bull, dragged him over near Dad, and threw the calf on his side. While Dad held him down, I gouged out the baby bull's tiny horns with the dehorning tool, smeared the wounds with tar, and gave him his shot. I reached into my pocket and pulled out my pocketknife. The blades had been honed with a fine whetstone, like Dad had taught me. The knife was ready for any appropriate use—snakebites, plugging watermelons, or castrations. I had watched my dad and uncles do this a thousand times.

For a moment, my mind wandered to the kind of talk I'd heard hanging around my Gregory uncles, Mother's brothers. Their talk was saucier, laced with cuss words, more about sex and fighting and stories of extreme practical jokes than was common among Dad's brothers. I had heard them discuss a man who had done something so unspeakable a bunch of neighbors had banded together and castrated him. I also knew about boys in medieval choirs who had been castrated before puberty so they'd keep their sweet, innocent-sounding soprano and alto voices. I had heard about men being kicked in the groin who were never able to have children, and I had been taught by my dad how to approach an animal to avoid being kicked myself. What I had not been taught, and the culture failed to provide, was a solid sense of assurance that a boy could survive into adulthood with his manhood intact. That thought might have caused my hesitation.

After a few seconds, I opened the blade of my knife. My dad instructed me to rip the bottom of the calf's scrotum so it would drain, push the skin up above the testicles, pinch the spermatic duct with my thumb and forefinger to retard bleeding, and cut the first testicle, then the second, and drop them on the ground. After I splashed disinfectant on the wound, Dad loosened the rope and let the little steer loose. He staggered a few steps, but steadied himself, seemed okay, and went looking for his momma, who was close by watching wide-eyed, blowing through her nostrils.

For a moment I felt dazed, as if I wasn't on the farm with the stink of piss and cow shit but was somewhere else, sheltered and quiet, watching a movie about a boy growing up on a farm in western Oklahoma. I shuddered. Something between my shoulders loosened and escaped. I stood up, staggered a bit myself. Muscles and bones seemed to have disintegrated. I felt light, as if I might float away. I grabbed hold of the top board of the corral gate. As the dizziness passed, I scraped my boots on the lowest board, making sure they were clean. My dad seemed to understand I needed a moment to collect myself.

I hadn't much of an idea what would happen next, except I'd catch another calf and we'd work them all, one by one, until we were finished. I knew tomorrow I'd plow the field where our dog lay unburied. I still felt sad for the collie, and for the buffalo that had been slaughtered, but no longer for myself or anyone else except my father who would lose me, his oldest son, to another profession more suited to my temperament despite how well I understood that farming is an important way of life.

THE BOX SUPPER

THE WOMAN WANTED TO ARRIVE EARLY, BUT THE MAN NEVER RUSHED through chores to go anywhere, not even to church; certainly not to the schoolhouse for a box supper. He thought raising money for the school was a good cause, that was true enough, but every drop of milk had to be stripped from the teats of four milk cows before he could turn them back to pasture and go anywhere. He did not want the cows to stop giving milk until a month or so before it was time for their next calves to be born and the milk cycle would begin again. So he was careful to take his time and treat the cows well.

When the man and boy finished milking and reached the concrete well house, the man poured the milk through clean burlap to strain out the flies. Once it was in the stainless separator bowl, he said, "Son, I'll feed the calves, and you can get cleaned up as soon as you finish the separating." The boy, anxious to finish his job, placed both hands on the crank, lifting then pulling down with all his strength to get the heavy mechanism of the machine to turn. When his breath came in gasps and he began to sweat, cream began dribbling into the catch basin.

The boy was glad he didn't have to feed the runty calves their powdered milk substitute. The poor pot-bellied little devils had been taken away from their mothers so the family could have whole milk for themselves and cream to sell. The money that came from the cream allowed the family to buy necessities they didn't produce and a very few luxuries, like store-bought toothpaste that made it easier for the boy to brush his teeth. Before, his mother had demanded he use salt and baking soda.

By the time the boy had rinsed the separator and walked to the house, his sister, who would soon be thirteen, had dressed their younger brother. The boy washed his own face and hands then pulled on the new pants his mother had ordered from the catalog. It seemed his legs had grown in the two weeks it had taken to mail in the order and receive the package from Montgomery Ward, because the cuffs of the brand-new pants were up around his ankles. He had fought with his mother about wearing them to school because to him they looked stupid, but this time he pulled them on with no complaint. He and his mother had compromised. He agreed to wear them five times, and then they'd be set aside until his brother grew into them. He had to wear them only two more times after this. She had already ordered him some new pants.

His mother came in from the chicken house where she had gathered the eggs. "Good, you're dressed," she said. "Now you have to finish your milk."

She went to the refrigerator, another convenience they managed to afford after the electric lines reached them last year, and pulled out a full glass of milk he hadn't touched at supper. "By the time I get my dress on, that glass had better be empty." She went into the bedroom.

The truth was, the boy didn't like milk, although he didn't mind the milk at his grandparents' house. They had moved to town, and a milkman delivered pasteurized and homogenized milk in glass bottles. With farm milk, the cream rose to the top, and when it was stirred, clots formed that felt like snot in the boy's mouth when he drank it.

He looked toward his parent's bedroom and saw the door was closed. He picked up the glass, dipped his upper lip in the milk, walked to the screen door and looked back again, then poured the milk on the cracked earth near the foundation of the house, leaving about a half inch in the bottom of the glass as he would have if he had tipped it up and gulped it down without taking a breath. As he placed the glass back on the cabinet, his mother came out buttoning her dress.

"Good job," she said, as she rinsed out the glass. "Come here, let's wipe that mustache off your face."

The last few evenings there had been clouds to the southwest suggesting rain, but the sky was clear as they sped over the state road and the sun slipped below the horizon. The noise of gravel pinging beneath the car made talking difficult, so they rode the four miles to the Garrett School without saying much. When they arrived, there were already two-dozen cars parked on the school playground.

Frowning, the woman said, "We're so late."

"They won't start on time," her husband predicted. Then he said to the kids, "It don't look like rain, but you kids roll up the windows in case."

The boy wanted to follow his sister who tripped off to be with her friends, but his mother grabbed him by his shirttail. "Come with me, young man, and bring the coffee urn. Remember, you're not allowed to play with the other kids."

The urn was heavy, but the boy lifted it out of the car trunk and followed his mother as she had instructed. The woman carried her supper box wrapped in a gunnysack. Inside the one-room school, she headed toward the curtain drawn across the stage the school board had built, even though times had been tough. The teacher had convinced them that drama, or "playacting," as the parents called it, couldn't be taught without a stage.

The women each brought a supper in a decorated box wrapped in a second plain wrapper. The boxes were to be unwrapped out of sight of the men because the husbands were not supposed to know which box belonged to their wives. Since the men would likely eat with someone else's wife, there was a naughty undertone to a box supper. Reverend Renfro of the Mountain View Baptist Church preached against this frivolity, citing a scripture: "Therefore a man shall leave his father and his mother, and shall cleave unto his wife: and they shall be one flesh." Despite her respect for Reverend Renfro, the woman had voted for and helped plan the fundraiser. County funds were depleted, and the school board had declared a financial emergency. There was nothing more important to the woman than the education of her children.

Mrs. McCune, one of the women in his mother's quilting circle, took the urn from the boy. Her hair was bobbed in flapper style and her lips slathered with shiny red lipstick. "My, this is heavy. Did you carry it all the way from the car?" The boy nodded, pretending it was nothing, but he was happy she knew he had done something difficult.

"You go back out now and sit with your dad and brother," his mother commanded.

The boy was not allowed to play with other kids for a month because, two Sundays ago, he had hit his cousin on the head with a croquet mallet after his cousin had knocked the boy's ball out of bounds. His cousin, nearly three years older, did not play football or baseball but was skilled at croquet. It was the boy's opinion his cousin played the game with so much intensity to make up for his deficiencies in the popular sports. He felt his cousin's behavior had not been sporting, was out of bounds itself, although it fit within the rules. His cousin, who won the game, could have left him with an outside chance, if not to win then to place second or third, but instead he had whacked the boy's ball over the boundary, costing him a turn. He'd done it out of sheer meanness. At least that was the boy's point of view.

He didn't want to sit with his dad and brother because it would be obvious he was being punished for something, so he slid into the corner where the curtain met the wall and watched his mother and the other women put the final decorations on their boxes. He still held out hope his mother would relent and suspend his sentence so he could play. His Aunt Zona spotted him.

"Hey you, you're not supposed to be back here. You go play with your cousin." She meant her son, the very cousin he had smacked with his croquet mallet. The boy realized that the whole incident had been forgotten, except that his mother remembered and held it against him. That made him furious. Before he could tell his aunt he was not allowed to play, his mother clamped her hand over his mouth.

"I told you before, go be with your dad. And stay there," she commanded. The boy still didn't move, so she pushed him. "Go on, get out," she said. "There are no men allowed back here."

"If I was man, you couldn't keep me from playing with other kids," he blurted.

Several of the women heard what he said and laughed. His mother turned her back on him and put her hands on her hips. A year or so ago, his parents had decided he was too old to spank. But if there was one thing his mother couldn't stand, it was a sassy kid. For that she might insist that his dad spank him when they got home.

He found his dad crouched near the wall with one of his uncles, Aunt Zona's husband. On the other side of his dad were some neighbors, Dootie Poor and Shorty Cook. His dad held his little brother on one thigh. His brother, approaching a year old, had not yet learned to walk. He was blond like their mother with very light skin. His mother was careful to make sure he didn't get too much sun. A few weeks ago, the boy had seen an albino man at the creamery. The man lived behind the store and did odd jobs for Jake Long, who owned the business. On the way home, the boy had asked his parents why the man was so white. They explained what they knew about albinos and about how they needed to stay out of the sun. That was why working at the creamery was such a good job for him. He could be inside where it was dark and cool until the sun went down.

The boy asked them, "Is that why you keep the baby out of the sun? He's an albino?"

"Of course not," his mother snapped. "He's light skinned like me, that's all."

His father had laughed, a deep throaty chuckle, and the boy liked the fact he had made his dad laugh, because the man didn't find many things funny. But his sister said, "That's the stupidest thing I've ever heard." He admired his sister, he thought she was beautiful, and her words stung.

"You need to think more before you talk," his mother said.

"I was just wondering, that's all," the boy said. "I don't see what's so wrong with that."

As he stood near his dad waiting for the box supper to begin, a girl he liked wearing a bright-yellow sweater ran by, and as she passed she bumped him, pretending it was an accident. "I'm so sorry," she said with exaggerated modesty. She finished with a curtsy then dashed off like she expected him to chase her. The girl lived at the Northern Natural Gas booster station and was in the sixth grade, a year ahead of the boy and more than a year older than he was. Beneath the bright sweaters she wore, her body had both slimmed down and filled out at the same time. Her skin was not sunburned with freckles like most other girls her age. She was brown and smooth, and her mother permitted her to wear perfume. The boy knew she didn't like any of the older boys in school, especially the only boy in her same grade, the youngest McElroy kid. Like the older McElroys, some of whom had gone on to high school, he wore dirty clothes that smelled. The one who was her classmate was a year too old for that class and bullied some of the younger children.

The one time McElroy had teased him, the boy put up with it for nearly a whole recess before he struck back and bloodied McElroy's nose. Although she knew he'd been provoked, the teacher made the boy stay inside for fighting the whole next day, two recesses and one noon hour. To temper the punishment, the teacher gave him a new book to read, one not numbered yet for the school library, a book about Teddy Roosevelt.

He had not told his mother he had been punished for fighting, but he did tell her how, later that same week, the teacher had asked him to answer a question none of the other kids—not sixth, or seventh, or eighth graders—could answer. It was the older kids' geography class, and he was not required to pay attention, although he often listened when the teacher taught not only the older kids but the younger ones, also. He was almost finished with the book about Roosevelt when the teacher called his name.

"Buddy! No one in this class can name the continents. How many can you name?" After he listed all the continents, he walked to the globe and pointed out their locations.

At recess, the girl from the booster station said to him, "You're a smart-assed little whippersnapper." He liked the fact she had used the word "ass." It made him tingle. She had risked getting reported to the teacher, so he knew she liked him and that she thought he wouldn't tell on her. He didn't know exactly what a whippersnapper was, but he liked the sound of the word. He didn't like it that she had said "little," because he was as tall as she was, though younger, and he thought he would soon be taller.

He told his mother about the continents and named them for her but didn't tell her about the girl and what she said about him being a whippersnapper.

His mother said, "Sounds like you're the teacher's pet."

He wondered what his mother would have said if she knew he'd been punished for fighting, but he felt pleased because his mother did not compliment him very often, although what she said did not sound precisely like a compliment. He didn't want other kids to think he was the teacher's pet, but he thought his mother might like it if he was, so he didn't deny it. He thought probably the teacher did like him and had kept in him at recess after he punched McElroy mostly so she could talk to him.

His teacher had told him that day about her son who went to another school, and said she wished her son could be his friend because her boy needed to learn how to defend himself. The boy did not tell any of this to his mother. He didn't think his mother would be in favor of a teacher who talked to a kid like he was a friend.

Since he was not allowed to mingle with the other kids at the box supper, he decided to sit down, but he didn't want to sit near Dootie Poor, one of the few bachelors in the Panhandle, because Dootie always teased him about having a girlfriend. He squeezed in between his dad and his uncle. His uncle smelled like tobacco. His dad never smoked, and his mother didn't allow smoking in the house, but the boy liked the way his uncle smelled and thought he'd probably smoke when he grew up. His dad scooted over to give him room and opened his arm so the boy could nestle against him. His dad's arm drooped over him, and its weight drew the boy up against his chest, and the man's chin rested on the top of his son's head. The boy gripped his father's forearm. It felt like a thick, braided rope.

From there, he watched the room, his cousin and the other kids playing, and his sister with her friends, and the girl from the booster station and her friends. He might have felt lonely except for the solid muscle and bone of his dad.

Shorty Cook said to his father, "Your boy's sure grown up."

"He claims he can work in the field this year," the man said. "Before you know it, he'll take over the whole operation." The boy knew that was his father's way of making a joke. Still, he felt proud. The boy had begged his dad to let him drive the tractor. Now that he was ten and had shown he was strong enough, his dad had promised.

Shorty Cook, another neighbor, who also squatted in the row

of men along the wall, had a cousin called "Boney" because he was skinny and had a prominent Adam's apple, but Shorty was called "Shorty" because he was tall.

Dootie Poor, a small wiry man with a smirking grin, was called "Dootie" because that was his given name. He was named Dootie by his own father because there were too many children to feed in the Poor family, but old man Poor said it was his duty to take care of the baby boy, so that's what he'd name him. Like a lot of other words in the Oklahoma Panhandle, Dootie was spelled like it sounded, not how the word was spelled in the dictionary. When he left home in his teens, Dootie dedicated himself to making money. He never wanted to be poor again. The boy's mother called Dootie a lot of names, for instance "windy" and even "dirty bastard" when she thought the kids weren't listening.

Dootie reached in back of the boy's dad, who had leaned forward as he talked to Shorty. Dootie twisted the boy's ear, pulled the boy toward him, and asked, "Who's your girlfriend nowadays?"

"Don't have one." The boy scrunched down to get away from him, but his eyes flitted into the room and found the girl in the yellow sweater. Dootie followed his eyes.

"Ah, yes, she's a cutie. Her momma's cute, too. And speaking of Momma, I've seen what your mother does to you, you little sissy, letting your mother kiss you. But I don't blame you, she's … a … real … beauty!" For emphasis he raised his eyebrows.

In farming, two men working together can do jobs one man alone cannot. Until the boy was able to work like a man, his dad and Dootie helped each other. The boy's mother complained, "I don't like having Dootie around the kids. He thinks he's such a charmer."

"He has new machinery. He's the best farmer around here. We're lucky to have such a good neighbor," her husband told her.

The boy had overheard Dootie telling stories about women. He didn't understand everything Dootie said, but he understood enough to make the boy think maybe he was a charmer. His mother claimed Dootie was nothing more than a windbag.

A couple of summers ago, Dootie did something the boy knew his mother would never forgive. He and two other men were helping the boy's dad with the wheat harvest. His mother had a garden just a few feet from the corner of the house. The native sod had never been broken until the man plowed it for the garden. Buffalo had undoubtedly chomped the grass that enriched the soil when it was turned over for the garden. The boy's mother grew beans, tomatoes, squash, carrots, beets, okra, melons, and even more.

During harvest, the woman usually took the noon meal to the field for the crew, but that day the men stopped the machines and came down to the house. She arranged the food on a table outside and set up a basin and towel so they could wash up without going inside. She didn't want the wheat chaff to fall off in the house. She served fried chicken and roast beef with fresh vegetables, including okra fried with small pieces of onion and pepper. Dootie complimented her on the meal, especially the okra, telling her it was the best he'd ever eaten. She was friendly to him that day because he was helping her husband get the wheat crop in when time was precious for all the farmers.

"It's been a good year for okrie," she said. "Normally it's a cranky plant, but this year is really good." She paused, looked at her hands, maybe searching for something else to say so she wouldn't seem unfriendly. "We've ordered some fruit trees. They'll be shipped this fall. In a few years, when we have fruit, I'll make cherry pie."

"You can bet I'll come over and help plant those trees to make sure I get some of that pie." Then Dootie added, "You sure keep a neat garden. Shows how much you care. You can tell you have a lot of love to give."

He raised one eyebrow, as if he hoped she might take it in a wrong way, but she passed it by as if she thought it was merely a nice compliment. She told him the kids did a lot of the work, which of course was not true, although the boy and his sister did help her with the hoeing. She started cleaning her fingernails.

Dootie stood up, handed his plate to her, and went out to look at the garden more closely. He walked down the rows of tomatoes, green beans, and staked cucumbers. He bent down, and when he stood up, his back was turned to the house so he was facing away from the boy, his sister, and the woman, who were all three watching him. His stance was odd, and he was doing something with his hands.

"What's that ridiculous man doing?" the woman whispered to her children. "It'd be just like him to pee in my garden." The boy didn't know what Dootie was up to, but he knew a man didn't stand that way when he peed. It appeared he was stuffing his shirt or something inside his overalls.

When it was obvious the other men were finished, the woman told the kids they could eat. While the woman was scraping the men's plates into a bucket, the two children ran to see what was left. There were plenty of vegetables, but of the meat only backs and necks and a couple of wings and some fatty pieces of beef were left. The boy knew he'd be permitted to have a breast, his favorite, when he was able to help with harvest.

While the children filled their plates, Dootie shambled toward the woman. He had one hand in his pocket and wore a cockeyed grin. Or it seemed his hand was in his pocket, but then it was obvious he had stuck his hand in the opening in the side of his overalls so it was actually inside his pants.

Just as the children returned to eat near their mother, Dootie stopped a few feet away from her. With his free hand, he unbuttoned his fly, reached in, and slowly, slowly, his eyes dancing with pleasure, pulled out a black bull snake he had found in the garden, three or four feet long, two or three inches in diameter at the thickest part.

The boy's sister screamed bloody murder and dropped her plate. It smashed into a thousand pieces. The boy's mother grabbed his barefoot sister, lifted her away from the broken glass, and pointed her up the steps and into the house. "You kids get to your room," she yelled.

The boy's sister, screaming and crying, headed toward their room, but once inside the boy turned around and looked out through the screen door.

Dootie held the snake just below its head, and as it writhed trying to get away, he stood in front of the woman, laughing, with his head thrown back. A bit of his shirttail stuck out of his open fly where he had dragged out the snake.

The screaming had startled the man, who had been dozing against the house for a moment. His ability to nap at odd moments helped him work the long hours farming required. Within a few seconds, he saw what had happened and headed toward his wife.

"You son of a bitch," the woman screamed and tried to kick Dootie in the crotch. He dodged, he was so quick and wiry. She missed, spun around, and sprawled sideways on the porch, her feet almost out from under her.

Still holding the snake, Dootie extended his empty hand to help her, but by then the man was there. He got between them, put his arms around the woman, helped her stand, and held her while she sobbed.

When Dootie released the snake at the edge of the garden, the man let go of his wife. She crumbled against the porch, talking to herself like a crazy woman. "I'll kill that son-of-a-bitch. I'll cut off his prick and stuff it in his filthy mouth." Then she saw the boy inside the screen door. "I said get to your room!" she shrieked. He ran as fast as he could to the room he shared with his sister.

Like the man had predicted, the box supper was getting a late start. The man and Shorty were visiting about the merits of planting different varieties of sorghum. Dootie grabbed the boy's ear again and pulled it hard enough to hurt. He whispered, "I'll give you a quarter if you tell me which box belongs to your mother." He showed the boy a brand new quarter.

A quarter would get the boy into a movie with more than enough left over for candy, but his mother would be angry if she had to eat with Dootie, and it wouldn't take much thinking to figure out how Dootie knew which box was hers. On the other hand, the idea of having the twenty-five cents appealed to him, despite the fact his mother would be upset. He also knew his father might see Dootie give him the quarter, and if he did, his dad wouldn't let him keep it. He had always told his son, never take money unless you earn it, and the boy knew giving out information he wasn't even supposed to know would not qualify as having earned anything.

The buzz of voices quieted when the boy's mother and the other women came out from behind the curtain. The men squatted on one side of the room with their backs against the wall while the women clustered on the other. Ralph McCune, the school board president, had volunteered to be the auctioneer. He wore new denim overalls and a bright-red shirt. He opened the stage curtain. To begin the auction, he picked a box from the table, not the largest and the most beautiful, but not the smallest or plainest. He held it up. "Now fellas, what are you gonna bid for this beautiful box?" He put it close to his nose. "I'll tell you, gentlemen, it smells delicious."

Dootie looked over at the boy and gave him a one-fingered wave, like when two trucks meet on the road and the drivers just wiggle a finger because they have to keep both hands on the steering wheel in case there's a strong gust of wind. The box sold for seven dollars. It was Aunt Zona's box, and Raymond McCune, the board president's brother and a neighbor of the boy's aunt and uncle, bought it.

Raymond and Zona sat down on a bench, their heads close together, apparently quite pleased with the pairing. Amid the clapping for the first sale, she opened the box, took out a dainty sandwich with the crust trimmed off, and with a big smile poked the whole thing in Raymond's mouth. He chewed, swallowed, and rolled his eyes back as if he'd died and gone to heaven. The women laughed, and the men clapped louder. Next to him, the boy's uncle coughed and cleared his throat. With the first box having brought a good price, the sale gathered momentum.

Some boxes went for as little as four dollars, while the largest, most beautiful ones fetched twelve or thirteen. Every time the auctioneer lifted up a new box, Dootie looked over at the boy and grinned, his teeth stained from chewing tobacco. He bid on a few boxes, but always stopped before the bidding ended. Once he held up the quarter so the boy could see it and polished it on his shirtsleeve.

The boy's father didn't bid until a purple box, not large but with an elaborate matching ribbon, came up for auction. "That's my favorite color," the man said. "Maybe it's your mother's." He raised his arm, but before the auctioneer saw his hand waving, the boy pulled it down. The man chuckled. "Maybe you're right, Son, maybe a little fancy. Not the way your mother would wrap something." The box sold for fourteen dollars. As the auctioneer picked up another box, the man said, "That one was a little rich for my blood, right, Son?"

Far more than half of the boxes had already sold when his mother's box was selected for sale. He couldn't help himself. He looked over at Dootie, who was already looking at him. He ducked down behind his dad's shoulder. Dootie turned toward the auctioneer and shouted, "Four dollars." When someone else bid, Dootie raised his bid by a dollar. The price went quickly to ten, then twelve.

"That's your mother's, right?" the man whispered to the boy.

The boy nodded. His dad put up his hand. When the auctioneer saw him, he bid thirteen.

"Fourteen," Dootie said.

"Fourteen fifty," the man said.

"Sixteen dollars," Dootie said.

Everyone in the room craned their necks to see who was bidding such high prices. The boy doubted his dad would bid again.

The man hesitated, then finally, "Sixteen fifty."

The auctioneer could hardly contain his excitement as he pointed back to Dootie. "The gentleman with the two boys is in at sixteen fifty. Do I hear another bid?"

Dootie's expression was blank, eyes half-closed—his auction face. The boy had seen it many times in the sale ring where men bid on livestock. "Twenty dollars." Disdain leaked out with the saliva he spewed.

The man paused to think things over. The boy thought the auctioneer would sell the box to Dootie at that price, but just as he called, "Going, going," his father bid twenty-one.

"Twenty-five."

Now people stared at Dootie. This was not about what might be inside the box, handmade sandwiches and pecan pie. This bidding was not between two neighbors helping the school board maintain an educational program. There was something unholy at work, maybe even Satan, who had once disguised himself as a serpent in order to trick Adam and Eve. Everyone knew Dootie, who didn't have a family to support, and always drove hard bargains, had enough money to support the school and to pay any price he wanted to pay, and they also knew the boy's dad couldn't afford to spend that much even for a good cause. Earlier in the bidding, the auctioneer had seemed thrilled, but now he appeared worried, concerned that he was involved in something he didn't understand but certainly something he didn't want to be part of.

"Twenty-five and a half," the man said.

Without pointing for another bid, the auctioneer stuck his baton toward the boy's father and shouted, "Sold, to the gentleman with the two boys for twenty-five dollars and fifty cents."

The room full of people who had bristled with tension relaxed with relieved shouts and clapping and yipping. They sounded like men driving cattle.

"Stay here," the man said as he rose to go take possession of the box he had purchased. The boy scooted his little brother firmly between his legs and put his arms around him, then let his chin settle on top of his brother's head.

As if he hadn't already guessed, the auctioneer held the box in the air and shouted, "Who's the fine lady that prepared this record setting box? Let's have her come forward."

The woman came from the side of the room with her long blond hair bouncing. She wore a print dress she had made for herself out of chicken feed sacks. The cut of it showed how slender she was. Her hips swayed as she strode toward her husband. In front of everybody, despite how shy she was, she stood on her tiptoes, flung her arms around the man's neck, and kissed him on the mouth for a long time, lifting one foot so the heel of her shoe pointed up, showing the only pair of nylon hose she owned rolled up just above her knee.

The boy glanced toward Dootie, but he was gone. The quarter lay on the floor where the bachelor had been sitting. The boy thought it must have fallen out of his pocket.

On the way home, his brother fell asleep with his feet on the boy's lap and his head on his sister's lap. The boy ran his hands over the Buster Brown shoes that once had been his own. The shoes still had good soles for learning to walk and had been polished by his mother so they looked almost new.

The boy noticed how his brother linked the three children, and how his mother sat close to his father, her head nestled on his shoulder, while his arm extended over the back of the seat, embracing her. The boy's hand drifted down to his pocket in the new pants that were already too short. The quarter was still there.

The boy felt the truth of how much his parents loved their children, and he sensed how difficult it was for them to raise a strong-headed boy like he was, all the while contending with people like Dootie Poor and even the girl from the booster station.

He couldn't see outside into the night, but he knew his father drove slowly. He could tell because the gravel didn't ping underneath the car like it had on the way to the box supper.

TWO-DOOR HARDTOP

When Dean found out his Uncle Bernie had to go to Korea, he went to his room and cried. Bernie followed him a while later, waited until Dean stopped snuffling, then said, "I have something else to tell Poppa. You're gonna like this part."

Dean wiped his face on his shirt. They went out into the parlor where Momma and Poppa sat listening to news on the radio. One American plane had been shot down the day before. The pilot was missing in action. Bernie ignored the news and told Poppa he was buying a new car. He had seen it at a dealer in Woodward, a two-door Ford Victoria, V8 hardtop.

"Wait 'til you get back, Bernie. You're leavin' in a month, and you'll be gone two years. The car'll be old, and you won't even have drove it much. You can draw interest on the money while you're overseas," Poppa argued.

Bernie said he'd saved the money to buy a car, and he wanted to make sure the money was spent on a car. Otherwise, all the postholes he'd dug for Dr. McGrew on the Cap O Ranch were wasted. He had a month to drive it before he left, didn't he? Then he turned to Dean. "Dean'll take care of it while I'm gone, won't you Dean?"

Dean said he would. He didn't want to disagree with Poppa, but he wanted Bernie to buy that car in the worst way.

The next morning, Bernie woke Dean up long before daylight. "Come on," Bernie shook him, "your momma said you can go."

"Where?"

"After the car, Dummy."

They walked in the dark to the highway at the edge of town and sat down on a culvert to wait for a ride. The road stretched east toward Woodward like a faint, gray ribbon disappearing into a clear sky that was just turning rosy. Dean had a thousand questions about what it would be like in Korea, about the car they were going to get, about what Bernie had said to Momma so she would let him go, because Momma kept Dean pretty close to home. Everyone knew his twin sister had died at birth and it had been considered a miracle around town that Dean had survived. Although there was Lela, who was older than Dean, Momma took extra precautions to make sure nothing happened to her boy. "A gift from God," she called him.

While Dean and Bernie waited for a ride, Bernie whistled "Mockin' Bird Hill," followed by "We Gotta Put Shoes on Willie." Bernie kept going back and forth between them, not pausing for a break. Dean wondered why Bernie only whistled those two songs, but he didn't interrupt to ask any questions.

After the sun came up, one of the Howard boys who worked at the stockyards stopped for Bernie and Dean and hauled them as far as the Laverne crossroads. They waited there until a semi-truck driver recognized Bernie and took them the rest of the way. Almost everyone knew Bernie. He had been an all-state halfback last year.

Dean told people that Bernie, who was seven years older, was his brother. It seemed to Dean like he was, but he wasn't really Dean's brother, he was Momma's brother, Dean's uncle. When Bernie was born, long after his parents expected any more babies, the Great Depression had made them too poor and too tired to raise another kid. They didn't send him to school when he got old enough for the first grade. Then when Dean was born, he was such a good baby; he didn't need much attention. There was just Lela and the emptiness left by the dead twin girl, so Momma and Poppa took Bernie to raise when he was seven. That was right after Momma and Dean came home from the hospital. Being the oldest in her family, Momma herself never made it past the eighth grade because she had to help with the young ones, and she wanted to make sure her youngest brother graduated high school. To Momma, there was nothing more important than education—except Jesus Christ, of course.

The two-door hardtop was forest green, with a white top and whitewall tires. Dean had never been in a brand-new car. The trip back home was like nothing he'd ever experienced. The smell of the car was so sweet there were moments Dean thought he might pass out.

"Feel down on the right side of your seat," Bernie instructed. "Feel that little lever? Push it and lean back." To Dean's surprise, the seat went back so far he was lying down. "In this car, you don't need to go from the front seat to the back. Don't need to open no doors so there ain't no lights comin' on," Bernie said. Dean pretended he knew why that was important.

Bernie kept touching the dash and the knob on the stick shift, and running his hands over the leather seats. "Son-of-a-bitch, son-of-a-bitch," he exclaimed over and over. Momma was about the best Christian in town, and she'd let Dean go with Bernie to get the car, and Dean knew he shouldn't listen to him because Momma wouldn't want Bernie to say those words. Bernie had been baptized and everything when he was ten but stopped going to church even before he graduated. After graduation, he got a job, and started paying a little rent to Momma and Poppa for his room.

Momma wanted Dean to be a preacher, a dream of hers ever since he survived those first few weeks, scrawny as a young rooster. And he crowed like one too, Momma always said whenever she told the story about when the twins were born. Momma said Dean's strong voice was part of God's gift. He knew he should speak up and tell

Bernie not to say those words, but he loved Bernie, different from how he loved Momma. How he felt about both of them was the same in one way. The feeling was not up in the top of his head where stuff he was taught resided but down deep in his gut where all of his most important thoughts seemed to settle. So Dean didn't say anything about how Bernie was talking because when Bernie left for Korea, Dean would miss him more than he could possibly imagine. Dean felt like he might cry again. He looked out the window so Bernie couldn't see the tears.

The first thing they did when they got home was test the car on the river bridge to see how fast it was. Rubber squealed when Bernie let out the clutch and again when he shifted into second. Dean knew that was a good sign. From a standing start, the speedometer needle hit eighty-one by the time the front wheels popped off the concrete onto the blacktop. Dean didn't know if it was the best ever, but he knew from the way Bernie let out his breath in a slow whistle it was a fast car.

They pulled into the driveway. The house was set on a deep lot, and Bernie drove to the back and parked on the buffalo grass. Dean didn't open his door because he didn't want to get out. Bernie looked over at Dean. "You're what they call my heir," Bernie said. "If anything happens to me, you get the car." Dean started sobbing. Bernie waited until he stopped, then they went in to eat supper.

Every night for the next month, Bernie took the car out. He never said where he was going, and Dean never heard him come in. Momma didn't even say anything to Bernie about staying out so late. He crawled out of bed about noon every day. Dean knew Momma took it easy on him because she was worried. It was difficult for Momma to see Bernie go overseas, even though she hadn't given birth to him. If Dean himself ever had to go, he doubted Momma could take it. But Momma said if Dean was a preacher, he'd be classified 4D and would never be drafted, except in the most severe of emergencies.

That didn't seem right to Dean. In the Sunday morning service they sang, "Onward Christian Soldiers" at least once a month. If there was a war when he was Bernie's age, Dean knew he'd volunteer even if he wasn't drafted.

In the daytime, Bernie and Dean took trips in the Crown Victoria. They went to Slapout, Fort Supply Dam, the Dalton Gang Hideout, the Alabaster Caverns near Freedom—wherever Bernie wanted to go. None of the places were very far from home, although Dean had never been to any of them. But it wasn't the places that made the time special; it was driving with Bernie, the hood ornament gleaming and Bernie sitting there with one hand cocked over the steering wheel and the other sticking out the window hanging onto the edge of the hard-top. Bernie looked around the countryside as if hedge apples, soap weeds, and a field of scrawny maize had become the most beautiful scenery in the world.

Momma, Lela, and Dean drove Bernie to the bus stop in Liberal. Poppa said he couldn't get off work at the grain elevator to go with them, but Dean thought maybe Poppa was still sore at Bernie because he bought the car against his advice. Lela didn't want to go either, but Momma insisted. Momma and Lela sat in the front. When they crossed into Kansas, Bernie reached in his pocket and gave Dean the car key. "Take good care of 'er for me, Dean. I'll be back before you know it." A chill crept down Dean's spine, worse than anything he'd ever felt before, worse than being in the cellar on a stormy night with salamanders sliming on the dirt floor, like once when the siren warned them there was a tornado. Lela and Dean had sat with their feet up on jars of pickles so no salamander could touch them while they waited to see if the town was going to be destroyed.

While Bernie was in Korea, Dean started the car up every day, let it idle, then revved it, pressing on the foot feed, gently at first, then a little harder until the oil gauge hit forty, then he slowly let it up just like Bernie told him to. Once a week he put it in gear, drove it forward, shifted to reverse, and backed it up. He made sure he didn't stop the tires in the same place because Bernie said if he did, they'd rot. When the gas gauge was nearly on the last line, he hauled the can Bernie left him down to the Conoco and used money Bernie gave him to buy gas. Once a month, Dean checked the oil. Every night he sat in the car thinking about when Bernie would come home, how it would be, the places they'd go.

He'd heard there were dinosaur tracks in some sandstone out near Black Mesa. That was more than a hundred miles away, but he knew Bernie would take him when he got back. That would be something. He wanted to see real dinosaur tracks. He'd heard the preacher say God created the world six thousand years ago. But from what Dean learned by reading encyclopedias in school, dinosaurs had to be older than that, maybe by a million years or more, so he was a little confused. He wanted to see the tracks first, then he'd try to figure things out.

One evening, Dean was in the car wiping out the dust, shining it up good—the silvery buttons on the radio and the heater, the latch on the cubbyhole. In the top of a cottonwood, a mockingbird trilled its evening song. Dean was thinking what a dumb song that was Bernie had whistled about Willie, a grown man who never wore shoes. Dean knew some of the lyrics: "He's a courtin' his cousin Tillie and whenever he milks the cow, he's a hummin' a song and a' milkin' too long, and a' gruntin' like a love sick sow"—just about the most stupid thing Dean had ever heard. He wondered why Bernie liked that song, but the music was kind of catchy, Dean admitted. He knew he should be going in. Momma would be looking for him.

He lay back against the leather seat. The surface glided cool and smooth on his cheek as he moved his head. Then he heard something. It seemed the words were coming from somewhere outside the car, just out of hearing, whispering on the wind: "Son-of-a-bitch, son-of-a-bitch." As soon as Dean knew he was the one saying the words, it scared him, and he stopped just in time. Momma came yelling for him to get back in the house because the sun was down.

One morning, Momma told Dean that Bernie was coming home. It hadn't been two years yet, but Momma said he was going to be discharged early. She told Dean he wouldn't need to start the car because Poppa had driven it to pick Bernie up at the Veterans Hospital in Clinton.

"Did he get shot?" Dean asked.

"No, he's not wounded," Momma said.

When Bernie came home, it was nothing like Dean thought it would be. Poppa said, "I took his car 'cause I thought he'd want to drive it. But he didn't. He sat over on his side and looked out the window all the way home. Didn't say one word. Not one."

Dean wondered why the car didn't seem special to Bernie. Sometimes Bernie drove it and they went places, but always just a few miles from home, usually over to Elmwood or Bryan's Corner for a coke. Dean never mentioned the dinosaur tracks out near Black Mesa. He'd checked a map and figured it was more than a hundred and fifty miles. Dean didn't think Bernie wanted to drive so far. He looked so empty, like he had left something from inside himself back in Korea, and as he drove, he kept gazing around, not as if he loved what he saw like he used to, but as if he was looking for what was missing.

A month after he came home, Bernie got a job at the pool hall. Momma said that was a bad place for him to work, but Poppa said jobs were scarce and a job's a job. Bernie started his shift in the afternoon, came home for supper, then went back to help rack balls until the last customer left, usually after midnight.

No one said much at supper, except things like, "Pass the chicken." If Lela or Dean said it, Momma said, "You mean, 'please pass the chicken.'" One evening, no one had said anything, hadn't even had time to ask for seconds, when out of nowhere, as if she'd been thinking about it for a long time, Momma said to Bernie, "Isn't it odd that you and Garrit was on that mountain in that same foreign country, the two of you from this one little town?" Garrit Hoover was Bernie's best friend from high school, the other halfback on the football team but without Bernie's speed. He was more just a blocker than a ball carrier. "It was the Lord's will," Momma said.

"The shells was explodin' all over the Goddamned place. He was only about forty feet away. There was nothin' but a hole when I looked over. Nothin' but dirt and a damned hole." As Bernie spoke, bits of food fired out his mouth like he was really angry or something.

Momma acted like she didn't hear Bernie take the Lord's name in vain. "I still don't see why they had to send you boys over there. Just what good did it do?"

"Edith, shut up about things you don't know nothin' about," Poppa said.

Bernie pushed his chair back and went to work. The screen door slapped shut harder than usual. Momma gave Poppa a withering look, then turned her face down and shut her eyes. Dean knew she was praying for them all: Bernie, Poppa because he didn't go to church, and Dean and Lela even though they had perfect attendance, but especially for Bernie because of what he'd said.

Bernie had been home two months when they drove him back to the hospital in the town ambulance. Dr. McGrew rode along to keep him calmed down. Dean fell back naturally into taking care of the car as he had when Bernie was in Korea. This time, Bernie was gone three months. The hospital wrote and said they would release him the next Sunday. They'd send him home in their ambulance.

Momma, Lela, and Dean went to church that morning like they always did. When they got home, Momma warned, "Kids, your uncle Bernie's gonna seem a little different for a while. I want you to go on and get out of the house until he gets in his room and gets settled. The last thing he needs is a couple the likes of you hangin' around and gawkin' while he's trying to get his bearings."

"Momma, let me stay," Dean pleaded. He wanted to see if Bernie was okay. Lela didn't care if she stayed or went.

Momma reached into her apron. "Here's a half dollar. Go see the movie." She handed the money to Lela. "You go on, take Dean with you."

Fuzzy Hoover, who owned the theater, usually showed westerns, a Gene Autry or a Randolph Scott. Dean liked the Scott movies best of all, but his movies sometimes contained cusswords, or almost cusswords, like "polecat," and when Momma heard there were bad words in a movie, she wouldn't let Dean go. When Lela or Dean wanted to go to a movie, they always had to tell her what it was, and she'd call the lady who worked at the ticket booth to ask about the language. This time she didn't seem concerned what the movie was. She just wanted the kids out of the house. Dean didn't like it one bit.

Lela and Dean plodded along on the new concrete sidewalk the town had poured after they ripped out the last of the old boards. Lela walked ahead of Dean. When he rushed to catch up and walk beside her, she slowed down and lagged behind, then turned around and walked backwards so her back was turned to him. Dean knew Momma wouldn't like Lela being impolite, even if he was her brother. They passed the *Times-Democrat* office and came in sight of the flat roof that shaded the front of the theater. It had the movie on it in big blue letters and they stopped to read. "THE GREATEST STORY EVER TOLD. The Story of Our Savior Filmed in the Wichita Mountains of Oklahoma." Momma must have known what the movie was all along.

A door opened across the street. "Hey, Lela," Dink Phelps called. Dink came out of P.O. Hibbs's drugstore waving at Lela. Dean thought Dink was mostly okay, though Poppa and some others in town were a little down on him because he had never played football. He was the star basketball player because he was nearly six and a half feet tall, and even with skinny legs, he could jump. That's why people sometimes called him "Jackrabbit." He worked for P.O. on Sundays after church and wore a white apron over his church clothes. Lela grabbed Dean's arm with so much pressure it almost hurt.

"We went to church with Momma," Lela said, "I'm not goin' to no religious movie. You go ahead, get your ticket, then give me the money left over. No, wait, that won't be enough." She thought a moment. "I know. Fuzzy's not there. It's just that old lady. She don't know you from nobody. Pay for a kid and give me the money that's left."

"But I'm thirteen," Dean insisted.

"'Course you are, stupid, but she don't know that. I wanna buy two cherry Cokes. Tell her you're twelve. That'll leave thirty-five cents. You can have five for candy."

Lela had always been excellent at math, but Dean knew that kind of answer was not what Momma had in mind when she sent them out of the house to the movies. Momma always said, "It's the hardest thing in the world, but you must always tell the truth if you want to be a Christian." Besides, Momma didn't like Dink, not because he didn't play football but because his family was Nazarene. She'd heard they did funny things at that church with their tongues and words no one understood, or at least they used to. More than that, Dean had been proud when he turned thirteen and had to pay full price for the movie. He stuck his hands in his back pockets.

"No-sir-ee-bob," he answered.

Lela grabbed Dean around the neck and dug her nails in. "Dean, I'm warning you, you little do-gooder. You better cooperate or you'll be sorry." She had a look on her face Dean had seen before. He knew she could inflict some pain. She'd given him a pretty bad Indian burn not that long ago. It wasn't that Dean was so goody-goody like she accused him, but he didn't want to do anything wrong on the day Bernie was coming home.

"I'll get you a comic book," she said. "Dink'll give me one they're gonna send back. P.O. don't keep that good a' track of everything."

Dean hadn't read a new comic book in months. "Okay, but if you ever snitch."

"Stupid, why would I snitch? I'm tellin' you to do it, and I'm older. I'd be in worse trouble than you." She had a point, though Dean knew it still wasn't right.

He stepped to the window and plunked down the fifty-cent piece. "One kid ticket," he said.

The old lady's hands, blue-black veins all through them, lay on the counter near the little slot where the tickets came up. The red letters that said "child" and "adult" had nearly worn off the brass. The woman's hair was mostly gray, with some black streaks in it like many old ladies. However, she wore glasses pointed at the edges, real modern, turquoise blue with rhinestones near the points. They appeared to belong to a much younger lady. The glasses made Dean uneasy. He wanted her to take the money and not get into anything. He knew he had to look her in the eye as if he was expecting his ticket right away, even if her glasses were strange. Their eyes met.

"You under thirteen, young man?" Her eyebrows went way up above those glasses, up behind her thinning hair that hung down in bangs.

"Yes ma'am," Dean answered.

The lady looked toward Lela, who was waiting for the change. Lela looked away.

"I know you," the woman said, "you're Bernie Parker's nephew. I could've swore you're thirteen at least. You're a pretty good-sized boy." She kept looking at Dean, then at Lela, as if she expected Lela to tell her the truth. Dean didn't know what to do so he waited, didn't say anything. It wasn't a hot day, but drops of sweat popped out and ran down his face.

Finally, she picked up the fifty-cent piece, put it in the drawer, pressed the child ticket button, and handed Dean a quarter and a dime. His ticket popped up right beside her hand. She tore it off and gave it to Dean.

"How is Bernie?"

Dean squelched a sinking feeling that stretched the bottom of his stomach. "He's comin' home today."

She looked at him for the longest time and just as he turned away, she said, "Praise Jesus. I'll tell Fuzzy. He'll be real glad."

It was like she'd hit Dean over the head with a hammer. Until that moment, he hadn't thought of it. Fuzzy Hoover was Garrit Hoover's dad. He'd lost his son on that same mountain where Bernie had been. "Nothin' but dirt and a dammed hole," Bernie had said. All the Hoovers had received to bury was an American flag.

Dean gave the change to Lela. She handed the dime back to him. "Ask her for two nickels so you can get some candy," she said.

"I don't want no candy," he told her.

She shrugged her shoulders, took the money, and loped across the street toward P.O.'s drugstore.

The seriousness of what he'd done soaked in by the time Dean sat down in the theater and the cartoon began. The old lady would tell Fuzzy that Bernie was coming home and that Dean had said he was twelve. He sat there, his eyes wide open, but he couldn't see anything, just the light flickering on the screen. Dean thought of nothing except the wrong he had done. Then the movie screen drew his attention. He saw Christ pushing himself up a steep slope, his sandals slipping on the loose rocks as he climbed the Mount of Temptation. On top, the wind blew his long hair so it streamed out from his head. The devil's voice boomed over the mountain, offering Jesus all the kingdoms of the world to rule if he'd fall down and worship Satan. Looking into the core of that powerful evil, Jesus said, "Get thee hence, Satan, for thou shalt worship the Lord thy God and Him only shalt thou serve."

Bernie was soon out of bed and up and around, and back to work at the pool hall, but he never drove the car again. Dean kept it in tune as he had when Bernie was away. Sometimes Bernie sneaked Dean into the pool hall, where Dean hung around with him, waiting until he and Clyde wobbled out of the back room. Then he helped Bernie home. Momma had the good sense to know Dean would never drink especially with such good object lessons about the sin of drinking right in front of him, so she let him stay up late to help Bernie.

Dean spent most of his free time in the car, just thinking about the places he might take Bernie when he was old enough to drive. They'd go see those dinosaur tracks for sure. Maybe even climb up to the top of Black Mesa, the highest point in Oklahoma, where the wind blew your hair and you could turn in a circle and see parts of five states. Dean wanted to know just what it felt like to be up there, what it was like to see so far.

One evening after school, as Dean crossed Main Street, Dink sped by with a honk and a big wave driving Bernie's car down the hill toward the river. Dean watched him until he came to the bridge. He winced when Dink ground the gears between first and second and the tires squealed. He ran home as fast as he could. Bernie hadn't gone to work yet. He was in the living room sitting on the divan, not doing anything.

"Dink tried the car on the bridge. He had no right!" Dean shouted the words, much louder than he'd intended. Bernie's head jerked back, like the noise bothered him. For a long time he didn't say anything.

"I sold 'im the son-of-a-bitch," Bernie finally said.

Momma knew Dean had lied about being thirteen the day Bernie came home, but she never said anything to him about it until he went to get his driver's license nearly three years later. By then, Lela had joined the Nazarenes, and Lela and Dink had a baby. After the baby was born, Momma and Lela patched up the rift created when Lela joined Dink's church. Momma drove Dean down to the courthouse for his driver's test. Before she got out to walk back home, she reached over and patted his hand. "Now Dean, you be sure to tell that officer your real age. He's gonna need to know you're sixteen for you to get your license."

Dean pretended he didn't know what she was talking about, pretended she hadn't carried his sin around three years without saying anything. "I'm praying for you, Dean," Momma added. He knew she wasn't praying he'd pass the test and get his driver's license. She didn't give a hoot if he passed the test or not.

Dean knew he'd never be as good a Christian as Momma, not even when he became a preacher. It's just that Dean was different too, like Bernie was after what happened on the mountain in Korea, and after Dean saw what the devil did to Jesus on the Mount of Temptation in *The Greatest Story Ever Told*.

Dean knew he had a lot to make up for. No way around it, he'd be a preacher, that was for sure. That had to be why he was alive and his twin was dead. Dean had no other explanation.

But first, before he went away to Bible College, he wanted to earn enough money to buy a new car, a two-door hardtop with leather seats. He'd gotten a job on the Cap O Ranch working for Doctor McGrew although he wasn't even out of school yet. Telling the foreman he was Bernie Parker's nephew was all the reference he needed because Bernie had been such a good worker. Dean wanted to take Bernie to see those dinosaur tracks and all the other interesting places they'd never had time to visit before Bernie went to Korea.

Photo by Julie Hanson Reiswig

FAIR GAME

SONNY STEPPED INTO HIS MOTHER'S KITCHEN, EASING THE SCREEN door shut behind him the way he had been trained. The room could have become a painting by Norman Rockwell. It was furnished with family possessions Emma Schultz had purchased at the liquidation sale after her father's bankruptcy and death. A porcelain rooster, statuesque and full-breasted, stood proudly on his shelf, his orange comb and white feathers dusted and shiny. The slaw graters hung in order from coarse to fine, while each pot and pan was polished to a coppery sheen. Emma stared out the window on the verge of a "spell," as Sonny's father called her hypnotic daydreams.

"Hey Mom," Sonny called. She jumped. After collecting herself, she lifted a bottle from the cupboard.

"Here's the ketchup. Where's Danny? Doesn't he want to eat?"

"Not on a game night," Sonny answered. "The team eats together after the game." A skillet rested on a front burner. Pork chops glistened from it, white fat riming the edge. "But Mom, you haven't cooked the meat."

"Oh, how silly of me. I'm sorry. I'll do it now." She turned the burner on, and after the meat started to sizzle, she stared out the window again.

Sonny Schultz and Danny Boone had been friends since early childhood. They had met at the funeral of a boy their age who had been killed in a farming accident. When they reached high school, Danny started staying in town with Sonny to avoid the long daily bus trip back and forth to the Boone farm, then Sonny stayed with Danny in the summer and worked on the farm with him. Sonny knew his mother cared for Danny as if he were Sonny's adopted brother, but he also knew she was not worried about Danny today like everyone else in town; the pressure of his first varsity game, all the talk about a state championship, questions about how he'd hold up under the pressure. Her concerns were for her Sonny boy. If only there was someone from the town who understood and could have comforted her, or someone from the church who would say something like, "Emma, don't worry about your boy, all he has to do is get the equipment out. He's in no danger. Jesus didn't command young men to play football. Jesus said 'Go into all the world and preach the gospel.' Look at the good he's done for the church. Football's just a game, Emma. Yes, good, wholesome fun for boys, but still, just a game."

Sonny watched her as she stood alone, gripping the edge of her scoured white sink. He knew she had entertained the idea that her husband might have been right. Their son would have been better off if she had shamed him, had ordered him back outside with Danny, to sweat, hit, run, until his lungs nearly burst. That way, he'd grow up like other boys in Cimmaron. Instead, when Sonny had come inside for comfort, she had hugged him to her breasts, kissed his dirty, tear-streaked face, and in that very kitchen with the mementos of her own childhood she had purchased back from the bank, she told him he didn't have to play football, ever, if he didn't want to.

Sonny knew how much she ached from those times when he was young and she had held him close—a vacuum between her womb and her heart. It hurt her to see Danny and Sonny together. Danny was admired, respected, and coddled by the community; her son, ignored. She hated those good citizens with minds that adhered to the Old Testament's idea of "an eye for an eye" and paid only lip service to the New Testament's more gentle "turn the other cheek." Her son, the water boy, was about to leave her kitchen for a game. Game? Some game, where boys in the bloom of youth can be injured, maimed, or paralyzed.

Every few years, a boy in Oklahoma died of heatstroke brought on by the extreme training regimens demanded by the most successful, sought-after coaches, like Gus Lipscomb and Cannonball Conner, the Cimmaron coaches. The Oklahoma sun could sap the life out of healthy young men, just as it had when the first pioneers pushed westward out of the green, forested lands east of the hundredth meridian into the short-grass, sun-seared conditions of the high plains.

Sonny knew the town owed his mother a compliment. "Your son is the best darned water boy this town's ever had." But no one said nice things about the water boy. Just the sound, "water boy," was derisive. Everyone else had reasons for being on the sidelines at football games—too old, flunked out of school, grossly overweight—but the water boy had no reason. He only had his excuses. He was scared. He didn't like pain and rough stuff. He lived the danger and excitement vicariously, hoping some of the glory would rub off.

While his mother worried about him, Sonny ate the food she had prepared and he worried about Danny. It was five-thirty, the time Danny had said he wanted to leave for the game, but Danny was not in sight. There had been a pep rally, and Sonny had lost track of Danny in the hubbub. Danny had not walked home with him. Then the screen door slapped shut. Sonny's mother jumped again. There stood Danny, tall, rugged, calm. No signs of pressure about the game.

"Where have you been?" Sonny asked.

"Nowhere."

"I thought you'd be here right after the pep rally."

"I'm back. I'll tell you sometime. Come on, let's go."

Sonny left his plate for his mother to pick up, and they walked out into the evening light. "Doesn't matter about the time; we're plenty early. We'll be a good half hour earlier than Coach wants the team to begin dressing anyhow," Sonny said.

"I like getting there early," Danny replied.

Sonny was not looking forward to the dressing room, the camaraderie of young men preparing for battle, bumping shoulders, snapping towels at each other's butts exposed by jock straps. "What's the first play you're going to call?" he asked.

"A halfback dive, left."

"Come on, why don't you go for a touchdown? I'll bet very few quarterbacks have ever done that, thrown a touchdown pass on their first varsity play."

"Coach told me to start the game with simple plays, get used to handling the ball in a game situation."

"That's what you'd expect a coach to say. That's what the other coach would do and what he'll expect you to do. They won't be ready for you to try a long pass on your first varsity play. Take a chance." The friends paused near the door of the old bus barn that had been converted into a dressing room.

"I might," Danny said.

"Good luck." Sonny forced a smile, and Danny smiled back. They were almost the same height, an inch or so over six feet, both muscled with broad shoulders from loading hay bales and scooping wheat in the summer on the Boone farm.

Danny reached and tousled Sonny's hair. "For luck," he said, and they stepped inside.

The heat of late summer lingered in the tin Quonset building. Before he had gone home for supper, Sonny had done his jobs, the details of a water boy's responsibility. He'd packed the medicine kit, bagged spare pads and tape, and completed a hundred other little jobs. There was nothing for him to do now.

"Come here, Danny. Let's get your ankles taped first off," Lipscomb called. As Coach finished the job, the rest of the team drifted in. "Everyone get dressed. Schultz, you got nothin' else to do? Walk around and help them," he shouted to Sonny.

Sonny's mind swirled. *Why am I doing this? Why will I be on the sidelines when the game begins? If I don't want to play, why don't I stay home?* Sonny reached up to help R.D. with the laces on his shoulder pads, but helping did not negate his feelings. *I'm larger than R.D. and many of the boys putting on uniforms. This is ridiculous, getting myself in this position. Humiliating.* He thought of the ribbing his dad must take from the other businessmen because his son didn't play football. He couldn't think of anything to get himself out of his dark mood.

He had stashed the equipment in back of the town ambulance that was always parked near the field on game nights in case a player was injured. Cannonball Conner, the assistant coach, asked Sonny to drive while he sat on the passenger side. Sonny flipped on the emergency light that reached with red fingers into the shadows of late evening. They drove in low gear ahead of the players and cheerleaders who rode a bus behind them. Sonny felt a little better. Maybe he was a vital part of the event after all.

They passed the wide concrete pillars of the main entrance for fans and entered a gate at one end of the stadium. Sonny kept the ambulance on the sideline while the team charged onto the field. The stands were not yet full, but the cheering swelled.

The stadium had been built in that optimistic time right after the war, with a seating capacity twice the population of the town. Though the population itself had not grown like the post-war boosters anticipated, the stadium had not been overbuilt. By game time, the seats would be filled by farmers and ranchers driving in from the countryside twenty or thirty miles from the town of Cimmaron. Latecomers would be forced to sit on the aisle steps.

The visiting team, the Shattuck Indians, dashed onto the field while their fans clustered high up into the stadium waving red pom-poms.

The Main Street merchants huddled in the front seats just back of the Dustdevils' bench. They'd heard the coach brag, and their hope had soared for a good season, maybe a championship, as they watched the practices. But tonight would be the real test of a team led by an unproven quarterback.

"You gotta admit he looks good warmin' up," LaFaye said. He owned the leather shop and was a talented maker of saddles and boots. "That boy's a natural. But you don't really know until you see what he can do under pressure. It's like Duffy," he said, jabbing Junior Goggin in his lardy ribs, "always talkin' 'bout what he'd do to her if he had hisself a woman. But if one points her tits at 'im, he hightails it like a scairt coyote." LaFaye punctuated his point by spitting out a wad of tobacco that landed on the grass not five feet from where Sonny stood watching the crowd.

"What?" Duffy Duncan said. "I heard my name." He was prematurely deaf from handling cherry bombs one Fourth of July when he was a kid. The firecracker not only burst an eardrum, it blew off two fingers.

"Nothin'," Junior said. "We was just talkin' about what a great lover you are."

Everyone rose for the national anthem and the prayer. The Dustdevils won the toss and elected to receive. Danny stood erect but relaxed near Sonny. After the "amen," he put on his helmet. "I better do what Coach said."

"Wait!" Sonny moved his mouth near the ear hole in Danny's helmet so no one could overhear. "Opposite End, Z Out, Flare Left. They'll never expect it."

The team spread like a covey of quail across one half of the field. R.D., a speedy halfback but light and easy to bring down, took the kickoff on the fifteen. A shoestring tackle upended him at the twenty-two. Not great field position. Buried beneath the excitement, Sonny sensed a faint hope for glory if Danny called the play he had suggested and it succeeded. On the other hand, a conflicting thought fluttered through the fringes of his mind: he might feel better if Danny failed.

The ball snapped into the fingers of the lanky, sophomore quarterback, controlling the ball for the first play of what the whole town hoped would be a three-year, record-breaking career. The play appeared to be a handoff to the halfback, the dive play everyone expected, but after faking the handoff, the quarterback pivoted and flared toward the team's bench, hiding the ball on his hip. Coach Lipscomb appeared stupefied. Sonny felt immense satisfaction. It didn't matter to him if the play he had suggested succeeded or failed.

Harley Pugh, the big end slated by *The Oklahoman* to be an all-state candidate, loped downfield, speeded up, and angled left in line with Danny. With a move so quick the crowd hardly knew it happened, Danny slid the ball off his hip and threw it, and it spiraled like a bullet. The ball settled into Harley's hands. It took him only four or five seconds after he caught it to lumber into the end zone. For those seconds and a few more, an eerie, disbelieving silence lingered over the stadium.

The speed of the play had stunned the crowd—then, finally, a spark built up force and traveled from fan to fan until the hometown folks burst with a frenzy unknown since the end of World War II. The fans fused to one another and to the team, but most of all to the quarterback who had thrown a football farther and more accurately than they had ever seen and had made the touchdown look so easy. Three thousand souls in the stadium were joined by that spark of common purpose—a winning season—to each other and to their brave sons on the field.

After the game ended in a lopsided victory, glorious hysteria fanned out into the countryside. Danny was no longer the son of a farmer, nor was Sonny just the water boy. Danny was the Dustdevils' quarterback, and Sonny was his friend. People stopped Sonny on the street to ask about Danny, invited him into their homes and shops, offered Dr Peppers and baloney sandwiches. When Danny and Sonny walked down the street together, they both drank in the admiration flowing from young boys who looked first at Danny then at his friend, their eyes wide with wonder that they, of all boys, should be near the quarterback, and if they could not speak to the quarterback because they were shy, they could speak to the water boy.

Coach had helped Sonny arrange a study hall the last period before practice so he could do odd jobs around the dressing room. On the Monday after the third game, Sonny sorted out worn pads while Hibbs, a reporter from Oklahoma City, and Coach jawed at each other about Danny's first three games.

"I haven't seen a performance like this from any quarterback since I've been covering high school football. You begin with the way he looks, so rugged country, even the way he talks, that drawl like a bull rider," Hibbs said. "Then he takes the ball, glides along on air, and suddenly cuts; you wonder, 'What the hell, why's he doin' that?' Then there's a hole, and he's through it like Moses parting the Red Sea."

"He's a special kid. That's why I took that chance and had him throw that long pass on his first varsity play. If any kid could ever do it, I knew he was the one," Coach bragged.

Sonny snorted and by accident dropped an empty bucket that clanged on the concrete floor. Both men looked over at him.

"You okay there, Schultz?" Coach yelled.

"Sorry," Sonny said

"All my coachin's paid off," Lipscomb said to Hibbs. "You can quote me on that."

Hibbs refused to let Coach take credit for something no one thought he had much to do with. "I don't think that kind of thing can exactly be taught. It's God-given."

"You're right in one way," Coach admitted. "We aren't dealing with your regular kid. This is a-once-in-a-lifetime kid. If we can keep him healthy, years from now people will say to me, 'I remember you.

You coached that kid who played quarterback for the Dustdevils.'
Coaches work their whole lives and most of them never get a chance
to coach a boy with this kind of talent. He's a career-maker. I might
even get a college job." Then he begged Hibbs not to print what he'd
just said.

Every Friday when Danny retreated to pass, everyone felt only by
the grace of God could anyone fling that stitched leather ball with
so much speed and accuracy. When he ran with it, his reverses and
deceptions created a kind of uncanny mass hypnotism. His opponents
all found out what Sonny had known since childhood when the two
of them played football in the back yard and Sonny had run in to be
comforted by his mother after a vicious collision. Danny was what
coaches call "a hitter." He never gave a tackler a clear shot, never
waited for anyone to hit him. He hit first, like a steel coil exploding,
destroying their timing, and as often as not, flattened the tackler
instead of falling himself. When he hit an opponent, it cracked like a
buffalo gun and left everyone stunned by his force. The fans learned
to imitate the sound with their mouths and hands. After each hit, the
imitations echoed through the stands and climaxed in spontaneous
applause. By every game's end, the fans of the Dustdevils' opponents
left the stadium shaking their heads. Sonny took note of their comments: "We didn't think he'd be quite that good." And, "I think that
kid might be an All-American someday."

Even the weather on game nights was unusual. Voluptuous sun-
sets blazed across the western sky, the dusty air laden with unbridled
energy. The cheerleaders scampered out of the bus, gliding through
the blue transparency of stadium passageways, black nymphs of darkness, then winged golden fairies as they flowed into the light of the
field. The crowds cheered them, too, pretty girls uniting fans and team
in the creation of glory.

Should not a minister have warned the town? Was it not wrong for
all spirit and hope to ride on the padded shoulders of a football team?

Where was Jeremiah when he was needed? Which preacher would explain it was not the end of the world if the team lost a game? Why was the town not reminded that all else pales compared to Judgment Day? But the whole town believed life simply wouldn't be worth living without a Dustdevil victory, and the ministers all came to the game vying for the privilege of offering the prayer spoken over the loud-speaker, prayers for the safety of the players, and prayers for victory, as if the nation were at war and God was being asked to choose sides.

The Monday before the most anticipated game of the season with the Boise City Wildcats, a perennial title contender and longtime nemesis of the Dustdevils, a distraction appeared in the form of two men who seated themselves in the bleachers the school had erected for the townspeople who liked to come out to the practice field and watch. The men were young and dressed like Mormon missionaries. Coach always approached anyone he didn't know for fear other teams might send scouts to watch the preparation. Sonny squatted down on one knee near the two strangers. Cannonball ran the team through their drills while Coach introduced himself to the young men. They told him they were from Texas Christian University and that the football department had heard about a couple of his kids, his young quarterback and the big senior end, Harley Pugh. Coach asked for their identification and said he didn't mind if they stayed so long as they didn't talk to any team members.

Slim Hall, owner of the Blue Peacock Motel, spread the word up and down Main Street. There were university recruiters staying at the motel. All that week, folks poked Danny on the shoulder, "Hey, I hear the universities are after you. Now be careful and don't take the first offer they throw out."

On Wednesday, the Christian Church minister showed up and watched practice. As the team trooped off the field heading to the dressing room, the preacher intercepted Danny. "Danny, God has led me to speak with you. I'll make it brief. I know you're tired after

a practice like this. But God has laid a message on my heart. Those
people at Texas Christian University don't believe Christ rose from
the dead, or even that Mary was a virgin. I don't know how they can
call themselves a Christian university. You must not go to a school
like that, Danny. That would be using your God-given talent and
your good Christian name to promote the liberal doctrines spread
by Satan."

Thursday, Coach practiced the team with no contact and called it
off early. He told the team, "These are tough guys we play this week.
They have a clean record just like we do. If we lose to them, we'll lose
the conference and our chance of going to the state championship.
I'm takin' it easy on you today because tomorrow night I expect you
to give back to me some real hurt on the field."

With plenty of evening light available, Sonny suggested to Danny,
R.D., and Harley that they go hunting. Sonny had never killed anything larger than a cockroach, but Sonny's father, a prize winning
skeet shooter who never had time to hunt real game, had taught him
to shoot clay pigeons at the skeet range. Sonny and Danny loaded the
guns into Sonny's dad's pickup. Full of confidence, Sonny told his
mother, "We'll have pheasant for supper tomorrow."

They met Harley and R.D. at the Cap O Ranch sign. Sonny had
his own gun, and his dad, who had a case full of guns, was honored
to loan a sixteen-gauge Remington to Danny. R.D. had borrowed a
gun from his dad for Harley, who had no money, barely had clothes
to wear, and got no hand-me-downs because he was so large.

Harley owned one thing—his motorcycle, the only means of
transportation for him and his mother. He claimed the bike had
been given to him by his dad, who worked in the Texas oil fields
down around Borger. However, no one in town had seen Delbert
Pugh in the flesh since shortly after Harley was born. Nor did anyone
think it odd that Harley and his mother rode a Harley Davidson and
Harley's name was Harley. It was merely their circumstances, no more

unusual than a hundred other situations any citizen of the Oklahoma Panhandle could name.

The four boys hunted in a wide circle around two sections of Cap O Ranch land. They tramped through bluestem grass, sagebrush, and sand plum thickets. Each time they approached the clumps of plum bushes, Sonny sensed the birds were in there. Any moment, the whir of wings would alert the boys to bring the guns up to their shoulders, and the air would smell of burnt powder. Sonny felt excited, anticipating a kill. He wanted to shoot a bird with blood and feathers, and flesh he could cook and eat.

There was time to think as they walked, and Sonny thought about his mother. Both her parents had been small children when they arrived in the panhandle, then called "no man's land." When Texas released its claim in 1890, for the first time the panhandle fell under a clearly defined rule of law.

Between 1890 and 1907, when Oklahoma became a state, it wasn't that difficult to accumulate land either by filing a claim through the Homestead Act or by earning money as a cowboy, a muleskinner, or gambling, and then buying land cheap from homesteaders who had been beaten down by the landscape's lack of generosity and its fierce weather. The homesteaders, sometimes men who came from a softer life or women who were left husbandless, were happy to receive even a small amount of cash for their property. In the case of Sonny's grandparents, Emma's mother had died, and Emma, the only child, stayed home to help her dad long past the time most girls got married. She and her father made it through the worst of the Dust Bowl, but the bank evicted them when her dad was unable to make a substantial payment on his debt even after a reasonably good crop in 1939.

Emma's father, discouraged and humiliated, had turned his favorite hunting gun on himself. It was then, in the middle of her grief, that Emma married the dashing bachelor who owned the local newspaper.

Everyone thought it was the trauma of her father's death that caused Emma's "spells."

After trekking nearly five miles, the four boys stopped at a windbreak, a double line of tamaracks and elms that protected a salt lick for cattle. Their shoe soles were glossy where they had been polished by the long tramp. They settled down to rest near the windbreak. The shadows lengthened, and so did Sonny's disappointment. Having never shot at anything except tin cans and clay pigeons, Sonny longed to shoot something swift and beautiful. They leaned their guns against the low branches of the tamaracks. Some roots were exposed where ring-neck pheasants had recently scratched beneath the trees. The birds had used the dirt for dusting their feathers and had dropped a few iridescent, bronze plumes.

Sonny picked up one of the feathers, drawing its edges through his fingers. Its silkiness reminded him of the yarn knots on the winter comforter his mother had used on his bed when he was a child. It was the same blanket that had been on her own bed through her motherless childhood. Their prey seemed to mock them, a scant few feet away, while they lay down to rest where the pheasants had scratched.

Through spiny leaves, the sky narrowed as the sun settled toward the horizon. Soft wind nudged the heads of ripe grass. R.D. and Harley talked of football scouts and girls, and of the victories so far this season. As Sonny rested and daydreamed, the whistle of wings startled him. A mourning dove, slender, blue-gray, darted and dipped then alighted on the top branch of the tamarack where they rested. The waning light brightened the pinkish wash of her breast. Her tail twitched as she preened. The others paid no attention. Sonny saw his chance. His hand wrapped around his gunstock, his finger eased onto the trigger. He released the safety with his thumb. The soft noise might have been a stalk of grass breaking, the dove's only warning. The blast sprayed a puff of dust where the gun butt kicked the ground. The shot tore through branches and leaves. The dove seemed to leap upward, and her wings unfolded before she landed near Danny. Startled by the shot, the other three boys stared at Sonny. Had he been there, Sonny's father would have called it a remarkable shot. Sonny had killed the dove much like a gunfighter shooting from the hip without taking aim.

"Bird flies near me, she's fair game," Sonny said. No one else said anything. Sonny stood up and walked to the dove. She lay in the grass, her eyes open, a wing askew. He picked her up. She was warm and limber. He closed his hand, leaving her head out as if she were wrapped in a thick quilt.

"Hold her while I get this shell out of the chamber," he said to Danny. Danny stepped back. Sonny looked at him, then at his other two friends. "Doves are game birds just like pheasants," he said.

He felt an odd mixture of emotions: pleasure over the competence that enabled him to kill the bird and remorse that her flash of beauty he had seen in the fading light would no longer exist on the prairie.

"One won't make a meal; what shall I do with her?"

No one answered. He squared his shoulders, spat, and flipped her away. As she tumbled, her wings opened. When she landed, a patch of tall grass supported her like a bier.

With great effort Danny stood up, walked to the dove, cupped her in his hands, and carried her nearby to a patch of buffalo grass, its seedpods hanging down like little church bells. "Any young ones she had can fly by now," he said. He pulled his pocketknife from his jeans. Near a staunch cactus, he sliced through grass roots to make a hole with steep, smooth sides. The others crowded in around him, but Sonny felt detached from the judgment Danny seemed to be pronouncing as he laid the dove in her grave.

With his brawny hand, Harley plucked some soft grass and lined the crypt. R.D. found a piece of bark, softened by weather, to be a pillow for her head. Danny covered the grave with a wedge of flat sandstone.

None of them looked at Sonny while they walked. When they reached the fence where they had parked, Sonny held the guns for them, barrels pointed upward as his father had taught him. One by one he handed them their guns and, after crawling through the barbed wire himself, he looked back at the windbreak, the silhouettes of the trees black against the sky. It was almost dark when Sonny and Danny reached home.

"Did you get anything?" Emma asked when they walked in. She stood with water running over dishes she had already washed. Sonny waited to see if Danny would tell her about his dexterous shot.

When he didn't Sonny told her, "We never saw a single pheasant. Hunting's not so good around here anymore." He tossed Danny an oiled chamois. Danny wiped the dust off his boots and walked out the front door.

Sonny didn't know where Danny had gone when he had disappeared before, at the beginning of the season. This time Sonny followed him with the same anticipation he felt while hunting on the Cap O Ranch. He jogged when necessary to keep Danny in sight and hid when Danny entered the back door of a small house. Twyla Lasher, star of last year's state ranked girl's basketball team, lived in the last house on the street. Beyond it there was only a barbed wire fence, buffalo grass, and soap weeds that stretched in the deep twilight to the river.

Near the river, the cottonwoods rimmed the sand hills, their waxy leaves dim in the after-light. Sonny watched the flowery, hand-stitched curtains flutter in her windows as darkness arrived. He felt like a child who had been left outside to play a game, Blind Man's Bluff or Mother, May I, while something splendid, far beyond comprehension, happened inside.

The principal dismissed school early and staged the pep rally on the school front lawn. The same popular girls led cheers. They wore short skirts with socks turned down. The shopkeepers had all hung up their signs: Gone to Pep Rally, Be Back Soon. The cheerleaders passed out chrysanthemums for a donation of fifty cents to support the squad. They burned an effigy of a Boise City Wildcat. Game time arrived clear and crisp. Sonny stood at his regular spot in back of the Dustdevils' bench, in front of the lower stands. He heard the comments of the Main Street merchants.

"He don't look sharp tonight," Junior Goggin said.

"Ah, he's okay. He's just warmin' up," Slim assured them.

Behind Junior, Slim, LaFaye, Duffy, and the others, on the first row above the far end of the Dustdevils' bench, Twyla Lasher, the best female basketball player ever to play for the girls' team, sat with her boyfriend, Brice Miller, the all-state fullback on last year's football team. He was on scholarship at Southwest Oklahoma University in Weatherford but had not yet lived up to his all-state potential. He had not even made the traveling squad, so he was free to drive home every Friday when the university had no home game and join Twyla in her little house at the end of the street toward the river.

Twyla exuded simple, hometown beauty. All the men who sat near the couple stared at her. A former teammate of hers, married and expecting, stopped by to visit. Less than a year out of high school, Twyla made a good living as a seamstress, a seductive mannequin modeling her own work. She wore a pink, loose-fitting man's shirt tucked in the denim pants she had tapered to fit her hips and legs. In a striking feminine touch, she had cut the sleeves of the shirt and then gathered them up above her wrists so they puffed out. Over her shoulder, she carried a hand-stitched embroidered denim jacket to put on when it got colder.

A wide-eyed girl skipped by, pigtails bobbing. Sonny could see her longing to be like Twyla, the wish to make rainbows with a bas-ketball that sighed through the silken net while the crowd stomped in unison on the hardwood floor, the nearest a girl could come to being anything like a football star.

As Sonny watched Twyla, his back to the field, she followed the moves of the young quarterback as he warmed up not far from the Dustdevils' bench. Brice put his arm around her and pulled her over against him. Sonny sensed how it felt to have been a hero then to recede into the crowd. More to Brice than a girlfriend, Twyla was a symbol of glory he had earned and didn't want to lose or share or forget.

It was the worst game of Danny's young career. He did not complete one pass, called the wrong plays for the situation, and could not execute anything more difficult than a handoff. It seemed he dreaded the hitting, although in other games he had reveled in it. The Dustdevils were behind six to zero. With under four minutes left, the Wildcats punted and pinned the home team on their own five, ninety-five yards from a tying, maybe winning, touchdown.

Sonny stood beside Cannonball Conner whose reputation as a master strategist had motivated Coach Lipscomb to hire him. "What are we going to do?" Cannonball talked out loud to himself more than he was speaking to Sonny. "We lose this game, they'll win the conference, go on to the state playoffs, and our season's over."

They both turned to look at Danny as he put on his helmet to go back in for a final try against a fierce Wildcat defense. He appeared dazed, disoriented, perhaps the result of the pounding he'd taken. If the team lost this game, there'd be little for anyone in the whole town to look forward to; no playoffs, no championship, only the second coming. But Christ was unlikely to return quickly enough to prevent the disappointment of a failed football season.

Sonny recalled how, a year ago, Harley Pugh, in the company of his best friend Brice Miller, had single-handedly beaten an oil field worker senseless. The man had teased Harley for dropping a pass in a game the Dustdevils had won easily. Harley's rage at the man was totally out of proportion to the insult. Coach's interference with the sheriff was all that prevented Harley from being arrested. A merchant had paid the oil field worker's medical bills then made sure the injured man left town.

"Harley's our only hope," Sonny told Cannonball. "Get Coach to move him to fullback and then make him mad. Maybe he can run over them just like he beat that guy up last year."

Sonny followed Cannonball as spoke to Coach. Coach called time out and waved Harley and Danny over for a confab. Coach grabbed the big end by the number on his jersey, pulled his face down to his own height, told him he was moving to fullback, and added, "You good-for-nothing poor white trash! Now let's see if you're as tough as you pretended to be last year when you beat up that guy who was half your size and I had to keep your lazy ass out of jail. I'm putting this team and this season on your shoulders. You'll be the hero. But let this team down, you'll wish you'd never seen a football field."

Next, Coach grabbed Danny and whispered in his ear.

The Dustdevils' short yardage play for the fullback had a simple name. This time Danny obeyed Coach. He called Bucket of Blood—left, right, then straight over center, play after play. No hiding the ball on his hip, no quick cuts and bursts of speed, no beautiful spirals everyone had grown used to seeing; just Harley's brute size and strength grinding out a few yards at a time. They punched him, kicked him, and poked at his eyes in the pileup. When the referees caught the infractions, they called penalties. Harley scored with ten seconds left, then ran the extra point over the goal to break the tie.

There was no victory celebration. The fans had exhausted themselves fearing the worst. They walked out of the stadium as if they had just attended a prayer vigil for a dying, unsaved man who had repented minutes before he died. Everyone hoped the season was saved, but doubts lingered.

No glory fell on the water boy despite the strategy he had suggested. Cannonball Conner accepted all credit. No one would have believed Sonny if he dared claim he was the one who suggested Harley be moved to fullback. Danny was so rattled he remembered very few details from the game. But some of the townspeople who were close to the field knew what had happened. Far in the future, some men will be sitting on the bench in front of the drugstore. One will say, "Do you remember that year the water boy saved the season? What year was that when he suggested the coach move that big end to fullback? That kid was poor as dirt. Rode a Harley. He won that game against the Wildcats when no one else could do nothin' including that All American quarterback. And it was the water boy who suggested the coach make the move. Duffy heard the whole damn thing."

"Duffy didn't hear nothin'. He could read lips, that's all."

"Well he heard the Schuster woman tell 'im she wanted to get married."

"And that's the last we seen a 'im. His nephew sold everything, sent Duffy the money I'm told, but didn't tell no one where Duffy went."

"Yep, that's right. I remember. Didn't tell no one. I wonder how he's doin'. I miss that ole cuss, even tho' he was always sayin' 'What?'"

The water boy never told anyone how heartsick he felt over the death of a mourning dove.

BRIGHT ANGEL TRAIL

THE LAST FEW SNOWY MILES NORTH FROM PHOENIX HAD BEEN slippery and stressful. After they unpacked at the hotel, the man and woman both took a nap, the woman on the bed and the man on the sofa. The boy turned on the television with the volume all the way down and watched reruns of *Bewitched*.

It was still snowing when his parents awoke. The boy asked his father, "Don't we need to check about the mule trip for tomorrow?"

As they walked toward the corral, the sun broke through the clouds, although light snow continued to fall. "This is just like it was when I came here that Christmas with my parents forty years ago," the man said. "It looks very much the same."

While his father talked with the guide, the boy looked at the mules. Most of them were brown or near black, but one was different, a yellowish-tan color with a black mane and tail. The boy glanced back at his father, who stood close to the guide. The men were gesturing as if they were having an argument. A cramp formed in the boy's stomach. A few minutes later, the two men walked over to where he watched the animals.

"So your name's Bobby. You pickin' out your mule?" the guide asked him. "That one I saw you lookin' at's named Andy. Buckskin. Unusual color for a mule. But first, you have to step over here so I can measure you. You're dad's under the two-hundred-twenty-five pound weight limit, even though he's tall and muscular, but you, young man, have to be at least four feet and seven inches before you can ride Andy down the trail. That's the rule. I was tellin' your dad, no exception."

The boy's mood dived. He hated it that his dad had tried to make him an exception. He'd been measured on his last trip to the doctor and was not yet quite fifty-four inches in his bare feet. For a moment, he hoped his hiking boots would make him tall enough, but even with them on and with the thick socks he wore, he was nearly an inch too short.

"Sorry, little buddy," the guide said. "We have these strict rules. But it will be a great day for a hike tomorrow. Just don't dress too warm. It gets hot when you get below the canyon rim."

On the way back to the hotel, his father said to the stunned boy, "I'm sorry, Bobby. I didn't remember the height rule. The guide said they've had it for years. He didn't know how long."

The boy, disappointed and upset, didn't speak until they climbed the steps onto the hotel porch. "I'm staying out here for a while," he said. After his dad went to their room, he studied the ornaments hanging on the Christmas tree. They had been given by visitors from dozens of countries. A man wearing a bellman's coat sat in one of the rough-hewn chairs watching the last snowflakes drift down from the brightening sky.

"First visit to the canyon?" he asked the boy.

"Yes."

"Goin' down the trail?"

"Uh-huh."

"Best way is the mule trip."

"I'm hiking with my parents."

"How old are you?"

The boy was ready for this question. "Twelve. I'm a good rider, but my mother was nervous about riding the mules," he lied. "That's why we're hiking."

"Too bad, that's the best way, the mules. But there's nothing like a good hike, either. Supposed to be beautiful tomorrow."

As he headed back to their room, the boy seethed. The rule about height seemed so unfair. He was angry that his dad had insisted they come to the canyon on the fortieth anniversary of his trip with his own father and mother. That also seemed unfair. If they'd waited, even six months, he'd probably be tall enough. He had no doubt about his competence. He had won the gold medal in the long jump for the junior high division in the Oklahoma regional track meet and had one more year of junior varsity track eligibility. Perhaps he could even win state, although he hoped he'd be promoted to the varsity in the spring. That would be even more special. If he was, Coach said he'd be the first twelve-year-old at Alva High School to make the varsity track team.

In addition to his athletic competence, he had ridden horses often on his aunt's farm in the Oklahoma Panhandle. He certainly was capable of riding a mule. The farm had been given to his aunt and her husband because the boy's dad, the only son in the family, had accepted a football scholarship at the University of Oklahoma, turning down his father's offer to be partner and heir to the farm. Every summer the boy stayed a few weeks with his cousins, who rode ponies bareback like Indians. The boy had good balance and the techniques of riding bareback came natural to him. He knew he was prepared to ride the trail. The whole trip had been ruined by what he viewed as ridiculous rules and bad timing. The words "no exception" still rang in his ears because he felt he was over qualified to be an exception.

Back inside the room, he asked his dad, "What happens if someone faints while they're riding a mule on the trail? Do they tie people's legs so they can't fall off?"

"You got me; I doubt it's ever happened," his father replied. Then he laughed. "No, I don't think they tie people's legs to the mules."

The boy knew it was a foolish idea, yet it had seemed logical in a way. His grandmother had low blood pressure and sometimes fainted. Yet from what the guide said, they didn't have any rules about low blood pressure. That would not prevent her or anyone her age from riding a mule down the trail so long as she was over four feet, seven inches tall and under the weight limit.

"It's just not fair," he said. "I wish we'd waited until next year."

The woman came out of the bathroom. "What are you two talking about?"

"Man talk," her husband answered, then said to his son, "Yes, any day now, you'll shoot up like a weed. But we're already here. We'll just make the best of it. The hike will be great."

It was the answer the boy expected, but it didn't please him. He wanted to hear something to indicate his father felt as badly as he did. He knew his father did not like having a son who was small for his age. Only recently had the boy started eating food of any color except white. "You have to eat something besides bread and pasta. A piece of meat! For God's sake, Bobby, please eat a piece of meat!" His parents both had begged.

He had stopped eating meat when he realized a chicken leg had once been the leg of a live chicken. His parents implied the lack of protein was why he was only in the nineteenth percentile of height for boys his age. He'd never said this to his parents, but he thought from what he'd learned in the science class he had taken in the summer that it was heredity. He'd inherited his shortness from his mother.

The problem of being small for his age was compounded when, on the recommendation of his teachers, his parents had allowed him to skip sixth grade because he was so far ahead of his class in reading and math. Before skipping a grade, he was already one of the youngest and certainly one of the smallest kids at his grade level. He had not been on a trip with his parents since the summer he jumped ahead because school breaks had been taken up with extra tutorials to make sure he stayed at the head of his new class. The Grand Canyon trip was planned for the Christmas break because his tutors, college students at Northwestern State University in Alva where they lived, also took Christmas vacations.

The boy first heard of the plan to spend Christmas at the Grand Canyon from his father, who told him, "I went on a trip to the Grand Canyon with your grandparents. It changed my view of things. I saw how big and wonderful the world was. I was your age, but my dad was younger than I am. I don't want to wait any longer to take you."

The boy had never met his grandfather who had died young. What his dad said didn't clarify to the boy something he'd wondered about. Was the plan for this trip made primarily for him, for his father, or somehow for both? The boy had the impression his mother was not in favor of it.

The next morning, the boy woke up first, opened the draperies, and stared out at the snow left by yesterday's storm. Heavy fog prevented him from seeing more than fifty feet from the window. For a few minutes, he remained quiet in the gray light then awakened his parents by making more noise than he should have while he dressed. Now that he knew they were hiking instead of riding the mules, he wanted to get started.

After breakfast, the man read the newspaper in the lobby while the woman went back to their room to sort clothes she wanted to leave with the laundry service. By then, the fog had lifted. The bellman from the day before was on duty, so the boy walked over and greeted him.

"It's a beautiful day for your hike," the man said. "The view's spectacular out there. You'll remember this day for the rest of your life."

The boy didn't know what to say. His disappointment about missing the mule trip was still palpable, and he didn't want to answer any more questions. He nodded to the man and went outside onto the porch to wait for his parents.

Half an hour later, they left the hotel. They could see the appalling

depth of the canyon even before they arrived at the beginning of the
Bright Angel Trail. Red-rock spires, cloaked in skirts of loose shale,
cast long shadows on the canyon floor. The beginning of the trail lay
in the shade of some large pines. A sheen of icy moguls, left when
hikers the day before packed the snow, had not thawed, although the
sun was bright and the temperature had risen a few degrees above
freezing. The woman asked her husband to hold her arm while they
walked over the ice.

"Look here." The boy pointed with the toe of his hiking boot.
"Today's mule trip has already left. There's a track."

"Hey, you could have been a scout for the US Cavalry," the man
said.

The boy was proud of himself for noticing the tracks. He wondered if he could have been a tracker in pioneer days. He loved stories
about the West, cattle drives, stampedes, and hunting outlaws.

At that point, the trail was ten feet wide or more and, although
icy, not slippery. The woman still shied away from the trail's edge.
When they reached the end of the packed snow, she asked her husband to turn loose of her, and they set out single file.

The boy insisted he had to go last, feeling it in his stomach. It
was not something he could identify exactly, just butterflies he felt
sometimes, like before his first rebuttal speech as the freshman whiz
on his school's debate team.

The man walked ahead, gazing out into the canyon. He wore no
hat, showing a full head of hair. He had a youthful face for a man
who was already past fifty. Over a plaid flannel shirt, he had pulled
on a sweatshirt with the letters standing for Northwestern Oklahoma
State University, where he was director of athletics. The shirt had a
hand-warming pocket, and he walked with his right hand inside of
it. He had strapped on a small backpack with supplies for their hike.

The woman, shorter than her husband by more than a foot and
a decade younger, wore insulated boots with fur around the top,

walking jodhpurs, a purple ski jacket with a tight waistband, and a fur hat with earflaps. Her hair, prematurely flecked with gray, stuck out in a nappy mass beneath it. She watched the path intently, using her left hand to grip the rock outcroppings on the canyon wall that rose, at that point, only a few feet above their heads. She placed her toes down first as if sneaking up on the step might make her feel secure.

The boy hung back behind her as far as he dared so he couldn't see the early gray in her hair. Her husband had once suggested that she use one of the many products available to hide her gray, but she refused. She was slightly more than five feet tall, and, in her tight pants, the boy thought she looked like a girl nearly his own age.

The Kolb brothers, early photographers who had helped popularize the canyon, had built their studio so that it stuck out over the canyon's edge. The building was supported by long posts so they could take unobstructed photographs. After the hikers passed the studio, the path widened and leveled off. Still, the woman's jacket dragged against the canyon wall that now rose above them more than a hundred feet. She brushed dirt off her shoulder and blotted her mouth with the back of her tan glove, dropping it quickly to her side to hide the red stains. She invariably bit her lip when she felt anxious.

Although the air was crisp and sound carried, the man got so far ahead of his wife and son they could no longer hear the sound of his boots. They walked a long time in silence until the woman called for her husband to wait. The man shifted from foot to foot until she caught up with him. The woman licked her lips, searching her husband's face, but the man was looking out into the canyon. Finally, she also turned to look out at the buttes and her gaze wandered downward, tracing the dark inner gorge that still lay in shadow. She glanced over her shoulder at the boy, who had stopped and stood near the outside edge of the trail looking across to the North Rim.

"Bobby, don't stand out there," she called.

The boy had expected her to say something, so he acknowledged her order by waving. The path was at that point about five feet wide with a sloping bank of thirty feet before it fell away into a sheer drop of a thousand feet or more. "I'm pretending I'm Andy, one of the mules," he said. "The guide told us they walk on the outside edge. Do you want a ride?" He leaped and threw his head forward like he thought a mule would if he bucked. His mother cringed. The boy was well aware of the diluted pleasure he received when he annoyed his parents with his, sometimes, boyish behavior.

The woman leaned against the canyon wall, apparently no longer concerned about smudges on her jacket. She clutched her chest with her left arm. When her son caught up with her, she said to him, "Don't do that! It makes me nervous." She pulled off her gloves and unsnapped her jacket.

"Let's keep going," the man said. "No reason to stop here." His left arm dangled relaxed at his side. His right hand was stuffed in his sweatshirt pocket.

"I think I'll feel better if I can go last," the woman said. "That way I can see both of you at the same time. This is so overwhelming, so large. I can't get over the feeling it's not safe."

The boy knew he couldn't object, but after they covered a few hundred yards, he edged toward the outside of the trail again, not as far out as he had before, but enough so he could see more of the canyon's depth to make the hike interesting. He had been watching his shadow, entertained by the way it lengthened or shortened as the trail turned first left, then right. As the trail veered sharply left, his shadow darted over the rim. Just his legs and torso were visible. His mother gradually fell farther behind. The boy looked over his shoulder to check on her.

"You have to stop it. If for no other reason, then just do it for me," she called to him. "I'll make it simple. Just … do … it … for … me!" She shouted the last word.

The boy had not realized how agitated his mother was until she spoke to him with her tone of voice. Now he moved away from the edge. The man walked back toward them. "We're in this place of total grandeur. Can you two stop bickering?"

"We're not bickering. He's scaring me," she replied.

The boy, trying to be positive, pointed across the canyon to the North Rim. "I can't believe it's fifteen miles over there. It feels like I could almost jump across if I could get a good run at it." They'd read that fact in a guidebook before they went to bed the night before.

"I don't think even the regional junior high champ can do that," his father said.

The woman squatted down against the rock, huddling with her buttocks on the heels of her boots. "I'm dizzy," she said. "I think I'm going to be sick."

Flexible from years of being one of the few certified yoga instructors in Alva, Oklahoma, she rested her head on her knees. After a minute or two, she leaned her head back against the canyon wall with her eyes closed.

The boy, realizing he had made matters worse, kneeled near his mother. He couldn't figure out what to do. Beads of perspiration glistened beneath her eyes and on her forehead. The sun, directly in her face, revealed the small wrinkles she always tried to cover with a light coating of makeup first thing in the morning. She justified using makeup by claiming it was an all-natural product and good for her skin, although she refused all other kinds of alterations or adornment, including hair coloring.

"I'm going back to the hotel," she said.

Now the boy felt horrible. "Please don't, Mom, you're doing fine."

"There's a rest stop up ahead somewhere," the man added. "Why don't we try to make it there, and then you can decide if you want to go back. Maybe we'll all be ready to turn around by then." He paused. "I'm in no rush to go back myself. These sights are even more spectacular than I remembered. I don't think I was old enough then to appreciate this place. Think of the first people who saw it. They must have fallen on their knees in prayer begging God to save their pitiful souls."

What his father said gave the boy some sense the man was trying to understand something. The boy wasn't enjoying the trip that much himself. Maybe he was immature. He was always getting that feeling. His dad had just admitted he himself had been too young when he came with his parents. The boy wanted to offer his mother some assurance he wouldn't annoy her any more. He could act more grown-up if he controlled his impulses. He couldn't find the exact words he needed to tell her, so he patted her shoulder. She caught his hand and kissed it and then held it against her cheek. He resisted the urge to pull it away. Her cheek felt hot to him.

"You'll have to give me a little time," she said. She let go of her son's hand, but her eyes remained closed against the bright sun. They let her relax, and her breathing eased. She took off her hat and stuffed it, along with her gloves, into the pocket of her jacket.

After a few minutes, the boy got restless. He walked down the path a few yards. He shaded his eyes with his hand. "Look, way down there, the mule trip from yesterday is on its way back up."

The woman opened her eyes. When she spotted the mule train, she said to her husband, "Remember those old Borax commercials?"

"No," he answered.

"From when I was a child," she said. "Twenty Mule Team Borax. They sponsored Death Valley Days. I know, I know, you told me. You didn't watch television. You were a serious young man." She smiled, not a whole smile, but nonetheless a signal she was coming around. She stood up and made sure her hat was secure in her pocket. "Okay, I think I'm ready. If other people can do it, so can I."

"That's the spirit, Elizabeth."

The boy, who had heard his father's coaching voice many times, felt the condescension. He threw his hands up with disgust, then realized that was not a proper reaction so he lifted them a few more times to make it look like he was merely stretching. He did not want to cause more trouble.

"I'll try going first this time," the woman said, "but don't get too close. You'll have to let me set the pace. I want to concentrate on the trail. You two will have to take care of yourselves."

"Sure, Mom. You can do it," the boy said, using the same overly enthusiastic tone his father had used. The boy heard it himself and knew his mother must have heard it too. He vowed he'd not say another word. He had to do something to prevent mistakes.

As they walked, the woman took off her jacket and tied it around her waist. The man and boy had dressed more lightly because the guide had told them it would get warm. "I'm beginning to like this," the woman called over her shoulder. "I can see more of the river. That seems to help."

"You've just got to be rational, that's all," the man said to his wife. "There are thousands of people who walk this trail every year. It's less dangerous than driving those narrow roads we take out to the panhandle. Remember a few weeks ago, Thanksgiving? You were driving. I looked over. You were going eighty. On those little roads, eighty!"

"That's ridiculous, Robert. You can see for miles, and there was not another car in sight. But I take your point seriously. I was doing something dangerous, driving too fast. Like you said at the time, what if a tire had gone bad?"

Since his parents were chattering away at each other, the boy gave up his own resolve to be mute. "I hope we meet the mules before we go back so I can see them up close." Neither parent replied. After their disagreement about driving in the panhandle, they now walked in silence.

Every few steps, the woman looked over her right shoulder down into the canyon. The colors were brighter now, light reds, many shades of lavender and pink, and yellow, clay-green and brown layers of soil and rock near the canyon's rim. No one spoke for a long time, but finally the woman said, "Robert, come in, Robert. Calling Robert, come in, come in."

"You said you wanted to concentrate on the trail," her husband said.

"That didn't stop you from talking to me," she answered. "You told me about the time I inadvertently drove eighty miles an hour. I'm sorry for teasing you," she apologized, "but we're on vacation. How about being with us? If that's not possible, at least tell us what's on your mind. And by the way, what's in your pocket?"

The man took his hand out of his sweatshirt pocket. His arms dangled as he walked. He slowed down, dropping farther back. When he finally spoke again, his voice was less edgy but more somber. "Our family only took that one vacation. My dad wanted to go to eastern Oklahoma, to see the Turner Ranch, the governor's world-famous registered Herefords. It was mother who insisted that the vacation trip not be a working vacation, that we see something really different. That trip we made here was the only time he was more than two hundred miles from home."

"I think I'm missing what you're trying to tell us," the woman said.

"All my dad ever wanted was that land. But the hardships killed him. Or at least helped." Before the woman could answer, the rest station came into view, and they were able to see the suspension bridge over the river.

"That bridge is still several miles away from here," the boy said. "Remember? We read it in the book. The distance of the bridge from the rest station."

They paused, looking again at the magnificent beauty, the deception of the distance. Then the man bent down to enter the small shelter, little more than a shingled roof that the canyon weather had worn thin. The woman and boy followed him. They sat down, and the man opened the pack and poured water for the boy, his wife, and finally for himself. He leaned back against a post and closed his eyes. They sat for a few minutes before the boy stood up, reaching then jumping to see if he could touch the beams that supported the shelter roof where it sloped. He was sweaty, so he pulled his shirt away from his chest, fanning himself.

"It's hot in here. Can we hit the trail again?" he asked them.

The woman stood up and tightened the knot in her jacket. She bounced on her feet, stretching the backs of her legs. "I'm ready," she said.

The man didn't move. Both hands were inside his sweatshirt pocket.

"Robert, I see you sitting there against that post, but you still seem to be a thousand miles away."

The boy stood near the shelter entrance looking out into the brilliance of the canyon, then into the shadows at his parents.

"I wish I had been a better son," the man said.

"How could you have done that? He didn't want you to go to college. That's the only way you could have been a better son to him— stayed home on the farm. But then you would have been a bad son to your mother, who had all kinds of aspirations for you. And she's so proud of you. Think of that. Your father was lucky his daughter didn't want to go to college and that she married a farmer. He had someone else to take over. In the end, he didn't even need you." Her voice had an impatient edge she had honed over the course of their marriage. She must have realized she sounded harsh. She softened her voice. "Are we moving on down the trail or going back up?" she asked him.

"I'm ready to go back." The man took his hands out of his pocket to rub his neck.

"You? Super-jock-dad-of-mine?" The boy kicked the rock floor as he gauged his father's reaction. "You just said how much you loved the hike. I want to see the mules. I'll show you. It's like I said, they walk on the edge of the trail."

After a pause the man said, "I'll go on if you want to."

The boy grabbed his mother's hand. "Come on, Mom, we'll wait for him outside." In a few minutes, the man came out of the shelter.

Now that they had rested and the woman had spoken her mind, she was radiant. She had a new spirit about the decision to hike the trail. "I think you're right about the grandeur. It's the most beautiful sight I've ever seen. That's why this canyon has been such symbol for the country. It's both grand and scary. Heaven and hell wrapped in one. It seems impossible that little, brown river cut out this whole thing."

The boy had written a short essay on the canyon for an assignment in school and knew a lot of facts about it. "It only took six to ten million years," he said. His mother laughed.

The boy wondered why she thought what he said was funny. He believed it was true, not a joke, and his reference book also said six to ten million years was a mere blip in the age of the earth. When he thought about getting older himself, becoming thirteen, he didn't think that was funny, either. His next birthday would be the first number with the word "teen" in it. He felt small and uneasy about his place on the planet. What was his purpose? He had asked about this in his Sunday school class, but his teacher returned to the printed lesson text without addressing his questions in a satisfactory manner. No one had anything to say about it, and he thought he was the only kid who wondered.

After walking on for a few hundred feet, the woman said to her husband, "I think it's very interesting that you're thinking so much about your father on this trip. You told me it was your mother who insisted on coming to the Grand Canyon. This trip was your idea for Bobby, remember? And I was reluctant. Now I see you were totally right, but you're obsessing about your dad, not your mom."

"What is that supposed to mean?"

"Well, it's just as you've always said, your father never did anything with you except farm work, was even reluctant to play catch with a football or baseball."

"Bobby and I do a lot of stuff together."

"I agree, you're a wonderful dad. You always think I'm criticizing you. We were speaking about your father."

The boy looked at his feet. He felt an urge to smile, and he pictured his face with the kind of grin he made when he had been caught with something he wasn't supposed to have or want, like the time he and his friend Eric had found a copy of *Playboy* and Eric's mother had caught them looking at it.

"Just don't make something more out of it than it is. I'm sad when I remember, that's all," the man said.

"Since he died so soon after you left home, you wonder if you killed him." She stated it as an opinion, not a question.

"Of course not. That's absurd."

"At least you learned a little bit from him. Enough to avoid being a bad father."

"You're hard," he said.

"I don't mean to be. But you keep yourself so aloof."

"I thought you agreed I'm a good father."

"You are, to a point, then you hold yourself back like your father did."

The boy couldn't stop himself from interfering. "Do we have enough water? I'm thirsty again."

"Yes, we have water." The man gave the boy a lid full of water from the thermos. The woman kept her back to them while the boy drank three cups.

They were low enough now there was little vegetation except pinion pines and a few sprigs of rabbit bush in those places where the trail sloped before it dropped over the rim. They came to a switchback and had a good view of the mule train a few hundred feet below them. The front guide had a full beard and wore a western hat that had once been white but now was streaked with sweat and grease.

"Let's make sure we're at a wide place in the trail for passing the mules," the man said. "Why don't we wait here? They'll be at this spot in a couple of minutes." He leaned against the sheer rock that rose above them, a hand still in his sweatshirt pocket.

"Robert, come on, out with it. What do you have in your pocket?" the woman asked her husband.

"Nothing." He took his hand out.

"This is what I mean, you share yourself, but to a point."

"It's just a coin," the man said.

"What kind of coin?"

"A silver dollar."

"Really? That silver dollar I've seen in your tie box?"

"I've had it a long time." He showed it to her.

"How long?"

"Before I went to college." His voice quavered. "My dad gave it to me. He told me it was the first dollar he made from the farm. He made sure he got it in silver."

"My God! This is the source of all the sentiment? I didn't know that silver dollar had a whole big history."

"This is what I mean. You impute more importance than there is. You think the worst. I don't have to tell you, or ask you, if I can carry a coin in my pocket. It's just a memento."

"No, of course you don't need my permission. But bringing that coin has infected the whole trip with your father's negativity. No wonder you're feeling uneasy. He gave it to you to remind you how you let him down by choosing your own career and life and not his life."

"Stop it, Elizabeth!" The man stood with his hands on his hips, glaring down at her. "I want to know, are you talking about me and my father, or are you talking about Bobby and me?"

The mule train was in plain sight less than a hundred yards away. The woman wiped her forehead with the knit band of her coat sleeve, which was still tied around her waist. Above them, where the canyon sloped up to the switchback they had passed, the last of the young aspens clung to the wall. There was some shade because of the rock outcropping, and the boy welcomed the coolness while they waited.

"You can't simply divide things up, get people in their compartments like you always want to. Stuff overlaps," the woman said.

The guide on the lead mule cupped his hands and called to them. "Lean back against the rock, relax, and don't talk." The woman and boy moved to comply. The boy watched the mules plod toward them on the outside edge of the trail, satisfied that he had been right about where they walked.

The guide's mule, a young animal recently out of training, was only thirty feet from them when the man, as ordered, finally leaned back against the rock with his hands behind him. As he did, a broken root protruding through a seam in the rock, part of the root system from the aspens above them, punctured the flesh of his hand. With a grunt of pain, he jerked his hand forward. The silver dollar he had folded in his fist fell onto the path and rolled toward the trail's edge where it sloped down then dropped to the plateau above the river.

The boy heard the coin, saw it roll, and dived for it. The young mule shied sideways. With the guide still mounted, the animal's back foot fell off the trail into the loose rocks, which gave way. The mule sprawled on its side in the shale pinning the guide under him. It happened in an instant, but the horror of it took more time. The mule kicked with its back feet to regain footing, which caused them to slide toward the precipice. The guide struggled to get out of the saddle as the animal thrashed harder, causing a cascade of the flat stones to fall over the edge. The guide got his free foot onto the saddle and pushed with all his strength, releasing his trapped leg. He grabbed hold of a small pine that somehow had found root in the rocks. The mule slid beyond him. For a moment the animal stopped at the brink and tried again to find footing, but its hind feet fell over the edge. The weight of its back quarters, caught in the force of gravity, dragged the animal downward and it disappeared with only the sounds of rocks rubbing each other as they slipped over the precipice.

The guide at the back of the mule train had dismounted and worked his way up the line, calming the terrified riders. "Stay in your saddles, stay on, stay on!" He turned the mules so they faced the canyon, their tails against the wall, then looked over the edge, where his partner lay clinging to the jack pine.

"Hell, Terry, I was hoping if one of you had to go, we could have saved the mule."

"Dammit, Buck, throw me the rope. This ain't no fun."

The boy, having seen the mule disappear, wailed in anguish, knowing he had caused something terrible to happen. The next mule flinched, and shivered. The rider, a heavy man, stiffened and grabbed the saddle horn yelling, "Whoa, whoa!" Buck put his hand on the mule to calm him and the rider.

The boy, scared and heartsick because of what happened, moved close to the trail so he could see if Terry was okay.

The boy's father kneeled on one knee, holding his injured hand. Blood dripped on the trail. When he saw his son move toward the edge, he yelled, "Bobby, stay back." He lurched and grabbed his son's arm, but the boy, in anguish about the mule, pulled away from him. The man's bloody hand slipped, and the boy went over the trail's edge, sliding in the shale.

The boy lifted his head to get his face out of the dirt, and Terry, the guide, came into view. Terry swung his leg out and clamped it over the boy. They were close enough to the chasm the boy had a full view of the canyon.

"Don't move," Terry said. "Don't put any more stress on our tree. The roots may not be very deep."

The boy clamped his eyes shut. He was scared to death.

There was no noise except their breathing as they floated on the shale. Despite the guide's instruction, the boy turned his head away from the precipice and opened his eyes. His parents were on their hands and knees, in shock.

On the trail, Buck spoke to the man on the first mule. "I'm using your saddle horn. You can leave your hands there, but hold steady. This mule won't move unless I tell him to." While he talked, he worked to untie his rope and prepare a loop. He threw it and missed. Buck recoiled the rope and tossed again. This time it landed squarely on Terry, who slipped the loop around his arm. Buck tightened the other end around the saddle horn.

"Son, remember, don't move. Not yet. Not till I say so," Terry instructed the boy. Keeping his leg over the boy's waist, the guide sat up. "Easy now, lift your arm, but easy, so I can get hold of your wrist."

The boy lifted his arm. There was dust caked in the blood left by his father's grip.

"What's your name?" Terry asked him.

"Robert."

"I'm Terry. Pleased to meet ya, Robert. Okay, Buck, pull and let's see what happens."

While Buck pulled, his partner, using the heels of his boots and one elbow, inched up the slope with the boy in tow. "I need a new grip on my little buddy before we try these last few feet," Terry called. "He ain't big, but he's difficult to drag through these rocks. How do you suggest I do this, Buck?"

"Dig your feet in. If you find anything that feels solid, I'll give you slack and you can use both arms to get a better grip."

"You can tell you've been to college, Buck. You're a genius."

"Having your feet on the ground is good for the thinkin' process."
Neither man smiled as they bantered.

"Don't move, Robert. I'm just changing hands. You prefer Robert,
Rob, or Bob?"

"Robert."

"You don't mind holding hands with me, do you? I'm not that
ugly."

In a few minutes, they were only a foot or two below the trail.
"You try to roll up the last step here. I'll push you from below," Terry
said, but the boy's parents grasped his clothes, making it impossible
for him to follow the guide's instruction. Despite the fact he couldn't
roll to help himself, his parents pulled him onto the trail, scraping his
arm and shoulder as they did. He grabbed the painful abrasion as his
mother folded him in her arms.

"Oh, Bobby, thank God, thank God."

The boy's father, very pale, put his arms around both his wife and
son. He held his injured hand away to prevent getting blood on them.
The boy's mother cried, deep unrelenting sobs.

"I'm sorry, Bobby. I tried to catch you," the man said.

The boy hugged him but did not feel like crying. They all three
leaned back against the canyon wall, getting their feet beneath them.
The boy's legs felt weak, as if he had just run a great distance. He felt
sad about the mule, the saddest he had ever felt about anything.

"I tried, Bobby, I really tried," the man repeated.

"It felt almost like you pushed me," the boy said. "And don't call
me Bobby, I'm Robert. That's what they call me in school."

"No, no," his father wailed, "I tried, I tried. My hand slipped."
He showed the boy his injured hand, the wound still oozing blood
on his palm and fingers.

The woman hugged the boy very tightly. "Bobby, your dad tried
to grab you."

"I tried," the man repeated. "I did try."

The boy knew the others were all watching them. He imagined they were angry at him and sad for the mule and were anxious to move, to change the scene.

Buck went mule to mule, checking with each rider to make sure they were all able to continue. When he finished, he brought his mule to the head of the line. Terry slapped his thighs with his hat, which had remained on his head through the incident. Dust billowed.

"One second," he said. He walked to the edge of the trail, balanced himself, put one boot over into the stones, packed down a foothold, and bent forward until he reached the man's coin. He picked up the silver dollar, stepped back on the trail and he handed it to the man, who took it with his bloody hand.

"Buck, I'll walk behind. First mule I ever lost," Terry said, shaking his head.

"Yeah, but you didn't lose your lucky hat," Buck said.

"Good thing or I'd have to retire."

"Well, you almost retired. Almost got a free trip, too."

Terry looked at the man, then the woman, then asked, "You folks want to walk behind with me?"

"Yes," the woman said. "Yes, okay." She stood up, put her gloves on, and tried to brush the dust off the boy.

"I'll do it," he told his mother.

She then reached to wipe his face, but he turned his head away, so she wiped her own brow.

One by one, as if nothing had happened, the mules started up the incline. Just like the boy had said, they walked on the outside edge of the trail, as near to the canyon as they could get. After the last mule went by, Terry followed, and the man, woman, and boy fell in line behind him.

The boy studied the canyon. The hues and vistas that had been so impressive on the way down the trail now seemed more ordinary. He forced himself to look ahead, up the Bright Angel Trail, to ponder the canyon wall that loomed monolithic above him. There was no more pull downward into fantasy, beauty, and nightmarish depth, only the challenge of trudging uphill to reach a place where he could walk free. It was as if the boy had not, before that instant, seen the canyon or anything else as it really is. He saw his life and his future more clearly—not the specifics, but he felt hopeful. He was growing up. He had not enjoyed the trip down into canyon, but he knew when it was over, he would enjoy having done it. If he ever had a son, and he supposed he would, he would bring him to see the canyon and take the trip so his son would have the experience. But he doubted he would ever feel the need himself to descend into the chasm again.

FREE LAND

My dad, the fourth child of fourteen—seven brothers and seven sisters—and my mother, the third child of eleven—three sisters and eight brothers—were married in the middle of the Dust Bowl. Dad was twenty-four, Mother was nineteen. Dad was a high school graduate, Mother had finished the eighth grade. Years later, when my sister was old enough to think about romance, she asked my mother, "Did you and Daddy go on a honeymoon?"

"Oh yes." Mother's face lit up with pleasure of the memory. "We drove to Darrouzett, saw the new steel bridge over Kiowa Creek, then had supper at a café in town."

"How far was Darrouzett?"

"Maybe ten miles."

Even in the worst of hard times, simple pleasures could be found.

The Reiswig boys were talented mechanics. Although work was scarce in the thirties, the three oldest of the seven brothers, Oliver, my dad (Fred), and Harvey, had found work on the Schultz ranch, a large farm/ranch operation near Follett, Texas. Their employers had assembled thousands of acres of cattle range and wheat land. Many homesteaders had tried to make a living and failed. They had believed too much easy optimism: "Rain follows the plough;" "A man's not much good without land." Ultimately, they left the land, walked away, and went back east to family, or west to California or Washington to pick fruit or become lumbermen. Maybe they received pennies for the land the government had granted them and for their years of labor on the plains, or just as likely they received nothing. Certainly there was no gratitude, maybe a handshake from a neighbor who was sticking it out a little longer. They left with little more than their own sense of failure, of being beaten by wind and heat, blizzards so violent the word "severe" was surpassed to such extremes it seemed irrelevant. The more introspective persons among those departing realized they had played a part in their own failure. Greed, ignorance, bad judgment—common human qualities had contributed to their own private disasters as well as to the national calamity culminating in the Dust Bowl.

On the ranch, my father and uncles were mechanics for the farm machinery and cowboys for the cattle. After my parents were married, my mother, Della, cooked for the ranch hands. Despite the conditions during the dirty thirties, Fred and Della saved some money so when the rains returned and the Dust Bowl ended in 1940, they put down six hundred and forty dollars to purchase six hundred and forty acres, a square mile of land, four times the amount of land given free to homesteaders. The Dust Bowl-ravaged land they borrowed money to buy was located ten miles east of where they had grown up on quarter-section homesteads across the road from each other near Balko, Oklahoma.

The first purchase after the land was a pinto pony named Skyrocket. Our father wanted to teach us kids to ride. Cowboys for the cattle, mechanics for the machinery; that's what he had in mind. While a well and a storm cellar were dug on the site selected for our home on the section of land, Mom and Dad, along with my sister and me, moved from Texas to be near the work. First we lived in a rental house on highway 270 that ran by our land that lay two miles east, then we moved into a vacant house my parents purchased for one hundred and fifty dollars from a suitcase farmer, Mr. Egbert. The Egberts had moved away early, after the first duster or two, and by doing so minimized their losses. When we moved into his house, Mr. Egbert must have been happy with the hundred and fifty bucks cash in his pocket. The house was barely habitable. Somehow my parents cleaned it up and made it livable. Later, they lamented the outrageous price they had paid for a house that had been unoccupied for years and had endured the assault inflicted by the dust storms.

When the foundation, well, and storm cellar were ready in 1942, a local family who moved houses as a side business to farming lifted the Egbert house off its foundation with everything we owned inside and moved it to our land. Following the recommendations of the United States Soil Conservation Service, Dad planted trees for windbreaks south and west of the buildings. He also planted one cottonwood tree to be the focal point for the front yard and three elms in the back for shade.

Ten years later, in the early 1950s, the trees were big enough to climb and the house had been remodeled and expanded with indoor plumbing. The farmland had been terraced to stop both wind and water erosion, and dams had been constructed on the most active creeks to stop the runoff and save water, just like Franklin D. Roosevelt and Henry A. Wallace, the secretary of agriculture, had recommended after their tour of the panhandle during the Dust Bowl. There were seventy-five head of cattle grazing the grassland, including a few milk cows, and some registered Herefords.

In addition to remodeling the house, Dad built a two-story barn with attached corrals and a large upper loft for storing hay. The first floor extended into the earth like a dugout home. The corrals sloped gently away from the barn for drainage. While working on the ranch in Texas, my dad had learned the importance of details and of having the right tools and equipment. He built a shop stocked with a welder, a forge, and an acetylene torch for repairing machinery. He added a garage for the car and a granary to store next year's wheat seed saved from the best of the wheat harvest from the year before. In two different poultry houses, Mother kept chickens and ducks or geese for eggs, meat, and down for bedding.

Dad was determined to mitigate the yearly gamble on whether or not dry land farming could grow enough feed to maintain and fatten the livestock through the winter. The United States Soil Conservation Service had been helpful and had subsidized the construction of terraces and grass restoration and windbreaks, but he went against the policies of the SCS when he decided to dig an irrigation well. The SCS claimed there was not enough water for irrigation anywhere in the panhandle. The federal policy for the area recommended returning all land to grass except the best of the best farmland, which should be tilled for wheat or feed for livestock, but on a crop rotation plan so that every year or two the land would lie fallow under a protective growth of soil-building, moisture-conserving legumes.

It was a complicated decision to make, to dig a hole large enough and deep enough for an irrigation well. A well with enough capacity would require casing twelve inches in diameter, so the hole itself needed to be bigger than that, at least eighteen inches. This was a high-risk gamble to find enough water. It required thousands of dollars of borrowed money. My dad first planned to employ a water witch to find the best place on the farm to drill. He knew of a man who lived on Kiowa Creek down near Darrouzett where Mom and Dad had gone on their honeymoon. The man used a willow fork to find the best place to drill a well. He walked around holding the willow fork out in front with the two points touching the lower part of his belly. The longest branch of the fork let the man know where there was a substantial water source (some said by dipping downward, others said by vibration). Many farmers who'd had trouble locating water vouched for the man. His success rate was reputed to be near one hundred percent.[2] Dad drove down to Darrouzett and found the

---

2   This was before my dad became an elder in the Christian Church. After that, prayer replaced everything that had divination or superstition attached to it.

man, but he found him drunk. My dad was a teetotaler and had no truck for people who looked for insight in a bottle. He returned home with a revised idea.

There was a windmill in the east pasture that pumped water for the cattle. The water went first into a stock tank, and the overflow from the tank ran into a small pond Dad had dug with an H Farmall tractor and an implement called a tumblebug. When he finished the pond, he planted a willow tree beside it. With plenty of water, the willow had grown to be taller than a man by the time he decided to dig the irrigation well. He found a good-sized branch with a fork in it and made his own water-witching tool. I wanted to walk around with him as he searched for the well site. He'd heard that a skilled water witch needed to be perfectly in tune with the willow fork in order to sense the tugs or vibrations. He explained he needed to concentrate so he'd have to do it alone.

When he returned to the house, he reported he'd locate the well site near the large pond northwest of the house.[3] He got a well driller to dig a test hole. The results seemed promising. A well driller from Kansas was hired for the big drill. It seemed to be a miracle that the drillers hit bedrock more than two hundred feet down into the earth and by the time they had, the early tests indicated they had found a water supply sufficient to pump over six hundred gallons a minute, enough to irrigate sixty acres.

My dad divided up sixty acres to meet different objectives. Twelve acres were planted to alfalfa that was to be cut, baled, and stored in the hay barn for winter feed. With irrigation, he projected he could cut and bale the alfalfa four times a season. With a one-wire electric fence, he divided twenty-eight acres into three small pastures that he planted to perennial grass and legumes so the cattle he wanted to

---

3   When I was older, my dad admitted to me he'd felt nothing from the willow fork. He decided to locate the well in the place most convenient for laying irrigation pipe both north and south in order to reach the maximum number of acres closest to the well. Logic and luck, and maybe prayer, over witchcraft.

fatten for market could graze on one parcel while the other two plots were watered. He allocated twenty acres to grow green fodder, sorghum, sudan grass, or corn that was chopped while it was green and contained its maximum nutritional value, then stored in a pit where it fermented and became silage, the ideal winter feed for cattle. For a year or two, the farm was almost like a tourist attraction as people came from miles around to see the irrigation system and the program Dad had designed.[4]

In addition, there was a pond stocked with catfish, perch, and bluegills for fishing. For us kids, Dad constructed a swimming pool with a sand bottom that was filled with fresh water from the irrigation well. The water was wondrously inviting in the heat of summer, so clear you could see twelve feet down to the bottom when standing on the diving board.

Details of the Reiswig family history are known going back to the 1760s because, in the 1980s, my family became involved in research to study genetic Early Onset Alzheimer's Disease. The research was conducted by the University of Washington in Seattle, which commissioned a search of records in Russia to find the lineage of our family.[5]

My earliest known ancestor, Johannes Reiswig, his wife, Catherine, and young son, George, were among thousands who left Germany for a year-long trip to Russia in 1766. They were tenant farmers in

---

4   By tapping into the Ogallala Aquifer for irrigation, my dad played a part in creating the alarming situation on the Great Plains today as described by Wil S. Hylton in *Harper's Magazine*, "Broken Heartland: The Looming Collapse of Agriculture on the Great Plains" (July 2012). The aquifer that took thousands of years to fill has been emptied in some places. And is still being pumped dry in others.

5   Reiswig, Gary, *The Thousand Mile Stare: One Family's Journey through the Struggle and Science of Alzheimer's*, Nicholas Brealey Publishing: London & Boston, 2010, p. 9.

Hesse outside Frankfurt—"serfs," as they were known then—at the mercy and whim of the often-insensitive noble land-owning class. The farmers dreamed of owning their own land and of being released from their slavish obligations to the hated landlords.

Catherine II, who would later be known as Catherine the Great, had offered German serfs free land beyond the Volga River on the steppes. They had to know in advance there were great risks involved in leaving their homeland to pursue dreams of land ownership in a different country. Johannes was fifty years old the year he left Germany and the fact he went voluntarily would be an indication of how unpleasant their situation as serfs was in Germany. As it turned out, things were not so great when they arrived at their destination in Russia, at least at first. The climate was not as mild as Catherine's promoters had insinuated, nor were there building materials available to construct homes on the treeless plains. The new arrivals lived in caves or any other shelter they could devise. Around twenty-five percent of those who left Germany for the trip to the Russian Great Plains did not survive the first winter in their new homeland. Johannes was among the dead from that first hard winter, but his son, George, survived.

Despite early hardships, the insular German community grew. To encourage them to settle the vacant steppes, Catherine had granted her German farmers exemption from military duty. This was important because young serfs, especially from Hesse, had been conscripted against their will into paid armies to benefit the nobility. Hessian mercenaries who fought for the British in the American Revolution were highly regarded troops. Since there was no fear of being conscripted, as they might have been in Germany, or drafted in their new homeland, the Germans in Russia married young and fecundity prevailed.

My family's lineage follows George, born in Germany in 1758, the son of Johannes who died the year he reached Russia in 1767. George begat Adam-George who was born in 1785; Adam-George begat George who was born in 1807; George begat Jacob who was born in 1833; Jacob begat Christian born in 1860. Christian was my great grandfather. All of these births took place in Walter, Russia.

The high birth rate became a problem. The amount of land was finite even on the steppes. The Russian government had made new allotments to the German communities in 1825, 1828, and 1840, but by 1860, when Christian was born to Jacob and Anna Reiswig, land was scarce.

In America, millions of acres of sparsely inhabited land had been added to United States territory in 1803, when Thomas Jefferson completed the Louisiana Purchase. Another vast territory was added after the war with Mexico. In the staircase of the House of Representatives in Washington, there's a twenty-by-thirty-foot mural, *Westward the Course of Empire Takes Its Way,* painted in the 1860s by a German immigrant, Emanuel Gottlieb Leutze. Leutze's studio was near the capitol in Washington. Abraham Lincoln viewed the painting and wanted to obtain it for the United States. The country paid half of the twenty thousand-dollar price, but the expenses of the Civil War intervened and the balance was never paid. The artist donated it. The painting depicts the movement of settlers from the East to the West that came to be known as Manifest Destiny.[6]

The United States Congress hoped to encourage settlement of public lands. That's why the government was interested in Leutze's painting. On January 1, 1863, even as the Civil War pitted state against state and brother against brother, people became eligible and started signing up for claims of one hundred and sixty acres of free public land as provided for in the Homestead Act of 1862. The Homestead Act required each claimant to build a home no smaller than ten feet by twelve and stay on the land for five years. When

---

6   This was the movement that conquered the country, subjected the land and resources to "the highest and best use," replaced native inhabitants with white Europeans, and replaced native animals with domestic bovines. Some believed this movement was inevitable and took place because it was the will of God.

those stipulations were met, title of ownership would be transferred from the United States to the homesteaders, who would then become owners of the "free land."

When the Civil War ended, the railroads expanded from east to west and vice versa in a great race, pushing Manifest Destiny at a faster pace. From American missionaries, the railroads heard about the restlessness among the Germans in Russia. Railroad representatives appeared beyond the Volga to persuade the Volga German farmers to immigrate to America, just like Catherine had asked them to move from Germany to Russia. The railroads had land to sell, and the country needed experienced farmers. The Germans also had heard about the Homestead Act from missionaries, especially Seventh Day Adventists. Many Germans in Russia came to American hoping to acquire free land.

In 1870 the Russian Government revoked Catherine's military exemption for the Volga Germans and began drafting their sons into the Russian army. That, in all probability, was the turning point for Jacob and Anna. Two years before their eldest, Christian, reached draft age, they came to America.

Jacob and Anna and their four boys, Christian, Heinrich, Jacob, and George, departed Walter, their village in Russia in 1878, and later that year arrived in Marion County, Kansas, on the Atchison, Topeka, and Sante Fe Railroad. They stepped off the train a few miles from where, only three years earlier, a band of Dog Soldiers[7] had raided and killed settlers. Despite that, the free land was in such demand, it all had been claimed by the time Jacob was in a legal position to file. He and the older boys worked for other farmers, biding their time.

I feel a strong spiritual connection to Jacob. He was the great-great-grandson of Johannes, who had left Germany for Russia in 1766. I am the great-great-grandson of Jacob, who left Russia for the United States in 1878. Christian, the eldest of the four sons, married

---

7   Elite, trained warriors of the Cheyenne Nation.

the daughter of another Volga German family in Kansas. My grand-father, John, was born there in 1883 to Christian and his wife, Mary Heinrich.

A few years later, unassigned land was opened for settlement in Oklahoma, the first of several land runs in Oklahoma Territory. It does not appear that Jacob and sons participated in the land rush. Perhaps the sons took over the claims of others who had made runs and held claims. Many who came for and obtained the free land were not prepared for the hardships of the Great Plains. Jacob and his sons had been equipped for Oklahoma on the plains of Russia. Jacob, Anna, and the youngest son, George, who was then about twelve, settled in the boomtown of Kingfisher, while Christian, Henry, and Jake found land to farm near Kiel, named after a town in Germany.[8]

In 1890, the panhandle, also called "no man's land," was added to the northwest corner of Oklahoma territory. By the time my granddad John was old enough to own land, the only parcels available to be homesteaded were west of the hundredth meridian in the panhandle. When the twentieth century turned, he moved there. In the panhan-dle, he found the same problem Johannes had found on the Russian steppes nearly one and half centuries earlier: no trees to build shelter. People cut slabs of sod and constructed sod houses, or they found an earth embankment facing away from the north wind, sliced a dugout into the bank, then constructed a roof out of anything they could find, echoing the family's early years in Russia.

My mother's side of the family had a somewhat different expe-rience. Great-granddad, Shadrach Gregory, had arrived in the pan-handle around the same time as my grandfather, John Reiswig, but with a little cash. The Gregory family, of Scottish descent, came to the panhandle from Harvard, Illinois, having migrated there from

---

8   Later the name was changed to Loyal when World War I began and the German population, who had maintained their own language during their sojourn in Russia and continued to speak German in the United States, was wrongly suspected of favoring Germany.

Pennsylvania, where they had lived since the American Revolution. How the first Gregory ancestor came to America is not known. It was not uncommon that soldiers conscripted into the British Armed Forces then shipped to America to fight against the rebellion saw opportunities in the new world for themselves and went AWOL. It may have been more than a coincidence that the first ancestor on my mother's side of the family was known to be in America soon after the Revolutionary War.

Shadrach's motivation for the journey into the high plains seems more vague than was John Reiswig's. It does not seem he had a specific need to get out of Illinois, like Jacob needed to get out of Russia, although the ultimate goal was probably the same: land ownership.

After filing papers under the Homestead Act, Shadrach ordered lumber that was shipped to Liberal, Kansas, where there was a railroad depot. He used a mule team to freight the lumber to his homestead, where he built a two-story frame house. Within a few years, he and most of the Gregory clan moved back to Illinois, apparently leaving the panhandle homestead in the charge of Arthur, my grandfather, who had settled on another claim nearby.

Around the time Oklahoma became a state in 1907, John Reiswig married Molly Schmidt, another Volga German, and my maternal grandfather, Arthur Gregory, married Alda Mae Carr, of Scottish or Irish descent. The Reiswigs and Gregorys lived on homesteads a quarter mile from each other a few miles south of Balko, Oklahoma.

The hundredth meridian is the eastern boundary of the panhandle and the western boundary of the larger part of Oklahoma, extending south passing near Childress, Texas, and north near North Platte, Nebraska. That boundary also is roughly the north-south line where the high plains rise out of the Great Plains, where the altitude is a minimum of two thousand feet above sea level, the sun hotter in summer, the wind stronger and colder in winter, and the average rainfall dips below twenty inches per year. There, on the high plains, west of the hundredth meridian, the families of my parents lived in the vortex where Manifest Destiny faced its ultimate test—the Dust Bowl and the Great Depression.

My parents purchased the farm on the heels of what has been called "the worst manmade ecological disaster in American history."[9] Despite their accomplishments, which I documented earlier, their travails continued. The irrigation program that was so innovative for the time could not overcome all trouble. Drought and dust storms came back in the fifties—not as bad as before, but enough to remind landowners that rainfall is fickle on the high plains. And hot! It was hot as hell.

During the first few years after the well was dug, the irrigated pasture rotation had been used mostly for animals being fattened for market. That year, when the natural grass on the range dried up and there was nothing else for the main herd to eat, my father turned the cattle loose on the irrigated pasture. The extreme drought and heat seared and wilted the grass and clover that had been made green with water from the Ogallalah. Something about the heat, the climate, the dust blowing in from other farmer's land, or something else, turned the irrigated pasture into a lethal poison for the range cattle whose diet had been dried grass with some supplements. Their digestive systems had adjusted to the drought, and were not prepared for the lush fodder. They bloated. We tried allowing them to graze only thirty minutes in the morning and again in the evening. That measure reduced the frequency of the bloat, but it was still a significant setback for the farm and for the irrigation program. We watched the cattle closely while they grazed. My dad and I took turns. If an animal went down, we sprang on the horse bareback, dismounting on

9   Duncan, Dayton, based on a film by Ken Burns. *The Dust Bowl: An Illustrated History*. The Dust Bowl Film Project, LLC, 2012, p vi.

the run with knife in hand. A slit large enough to get one arm into the cow's stomach was cut to relieve the pressure of gas. Despite our efforts, over the course of the summer, one third of the cattle died, and another third had holes in their sides that we treated far into the fall to keep out the maggots.

Less than twenty years after the irrigation well was dug, my father became so ill with early onset Alzheimer's disease he and my mother were no longer able to run the farm. My brother and I had left the farm to pursue the life our mother had so hoped for us when she gave us music lessons and exposed us to every educational and cultural advantage she could find. My brother and I both earned PhDs. My sister enjoyed the same opportunities my mother gave her boys, but she and her husband had stayed in the panhandle and were prepared to take over the farm when my dad was unable to work.

After my father died, Mother moved to town. She enjoyed town life. She worked with the church, had friends, and saw grandchildren and great-grandchildren. In her mid-seventies, she suffered a stroke. I made monthly trips to see her in the nursing home. As I flew from New York to Oklahoma, I read the literature about Manifest Destiny and the early Oklahoma settlers of the nineteenth and twentieth centuries. I was impressed by their optimism and relative prosperity, especially before the Dust Bowl. On those lonely, two-hundred-mile drives from Oklahoma City to the panhandle, I thought about the stories that my two sets of grandparents, my uncles and aunts, and my own parents had told. The route I followed west out of Oklahoma City was the same route many settlers had followed on their journeys west. They knew little or nothing about the concept or philosophy of Manifest Destiny. They were only looking for land.

West on I-40 out of the Oklahoma capitol city, the country is flat with a few rolling hills. When you leave the interstate to head northwest on Route 270, the same highway that ran by our farm, the car strains. Although the land looks flat, with low hills and valleys that break the monotony, the drive is gradually uphill until you pass Woodward. A few miles west of Woodward comes Fort Supply, where George Armstrong Custer provisioned his troops for that wintery trek in 1868 when he and the US Cavalry attacked the village of Black Kettle on the Washita River. Black Kettle was no longer a Cheyenne warrior. He spoke to his nation advocating peace and compromise. The buckskin-clad Custer and his troopers killed Black Kettle and, they claimed, one hundred three Cheyenne warriors. The Cheyenne people agreed that number of their people had died, but numbered only eleven dead men, the old peace chief included, while the others killed were women and children. Not long after, Custer was declared to be a national hero. In that ignoble declaration, westward the course of empire did take its way and it did not wane until the last Native American was sent to a reservation or consumed into the white culture and the Oklahoma Panhandle finally came under the plough. Manifest Destiny had conquered its last outpost.

West of Fort Supply, something happens to the landscape. There's sagebrush but few trees. As you near the hundredth meridian, you feel a sensation in the car similar to that of an airplane leveling after reaching the altitude for its flight. You are then on the high plains, the Oklahoma Panhandle.

On one of those trips when I was visiting Mother in the nursing home, on the morning of the day I had to return New York, we had planned one more drive into the countryside. This was our indulgence—to drive by all the places she, my dad, and our family, including my grand parents, had lived. I'd name the people I thought had once lived in the places whether they were vacant or currently occupied. She'd shake her head, yes or no. If she said no, I racked my brain and guessed again who had lived there. These truly had been Jefferson's yeoman farmers, those who had not only homesteaded within the Louisiana Purchase but had survived the disaster of the thirties.

After getting her in the car and storing her wheelchair in the trunk on this particular day, we drove into the country. It was a startling, brilliant day—sun, gentle wind, green grass and wheat because of spring rains. The air smelled so good it seemed as if it could heal any illness. On my shoulders, however, hung a shroud of sadness, knowing my mother was failing. This trip or another one like it would be the last time I'd see her alive.

We returned to the nursing home nearly two hours later. As I wheeled her past the nurses' station, the odor of disinfectant and soiled bedding hung in the air. The astringency was extra irritating because we had been out and away from it and were no longer acclimatized. But the smell was familiar, not just from earlier in the morning before we left, but something from long ago. From the frail, bent figure who could not speak I heard a word. She only communicated with gestures using her one good arm and hand. I stopped and kneeled down on one knee in front of her so I was eye to eye. Had I actually heard her say a word?

"Did you say 'barn'?"

She nodded. I started to laugh. Through my sadness, because of my sadness, the laughing got out of control, and Mother laughed with me, one of those deep-gut, burden-releasing, can't-stop-laughing laughs. Nurses stopped by with quizzical looks, but I couldn't explain, our laughing was so extreme. Some of them laughed with us.

As we wheeled down the hall, the odors had reminded us both of the dairy barn where extreme cleanliness and germ control was required. After the cows had been milked and the floors had been scrubbed with disinfectant, the barn had smelled just like the nursing home.

My parents were fortunate to turn the farm over to one of their children. That arrangement lasted another generation until my sister, who suffered from early onset Alzheimer's Disease, died in the same nursing home shortly after my mother. A couple years later my brother-in-law slipped, hit his head as he climbed down from the combine, and died without regaining consciousness. None of their three sons wanted to farm.

My father and sister were the last farmers in the line of farmers for eleven known generations in the Reiswig family that extended backward from the Oklahoma Panhandle, to the steppes of Russia, to the Hessian countryside near Frankfurt, Germany.

From the fourteen siblings in my dad's family and eleven in my mother's, one cousin remains on a farm in Western Oklahoma, the last farming descendant from my family who moved west propelled by the forces of Manifest Destiny to participate in the last great land rush.

Map I

COLORADO • NEW MEXICO • KANSAS ②⑧ ↑ 50 mi • OKLAHOMA • MISSOURI • ⑤ ↓ 60 mi • High plains • Great plains • TEXAS • Oklahoma City • Hundredth Meridian • ARKANSAS • ⑯ • ↓ 80 mi ②⑤ • TEXAS

Alabaster Caverns M3-1
Alva M3-2
Balko M2-3
Black Mesa M2-4
Boise City M2-5
Borger M1-6
Bryans Corner M2-7
Cap O Ranch M2-8
Clinton M3-9
Dalton Gang Hideout M2-10
Freedom M3-11
Follett M2-12
Fort Supply M3-13
Garrett School M2-14
Hooker M2-15
Hundredth Meridian M H6
Keil (Loyal) M3-17

Kingfisher M3-18
Laverne M3-19
Liberal M2-20
Mountain View M2-21
the Oklahoman M3-22
Shattuck M3-23
Slapout M3-24
Ten Miles E of Balko M2-24
TCU M1-25
Un. of Okla M3-26
Weatherford M3-27
Wichita M1-28
Wichita Mt. Refuge M3-29
Woodward M3-30

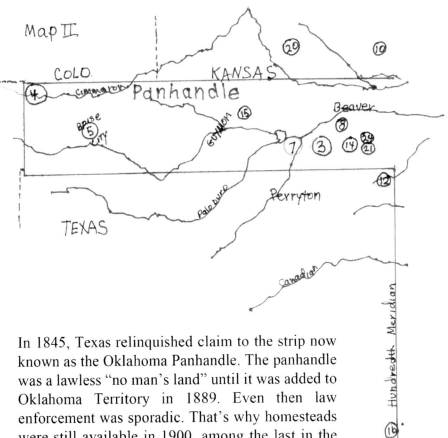

Map II.

COLO.   KANSAS
Panhandle
Cimarron
Boise City
Goodwell
Beaver
TEXAS
Palo Duro   Perryton
Canadian
Hundredth Meridian

In 1845, Texas relinquished claim to the strip now known as the Oklahoma Panhandle. The panhandle was a lawless "no man's land" until it was added to Oklahoma Territory in 1889. Even then law enforcement was sporadic. That's why homesteads were still available in 1900, among the last in the U.S. And, then, the Reiswigs and Gregorys arrived to claim their "free land."

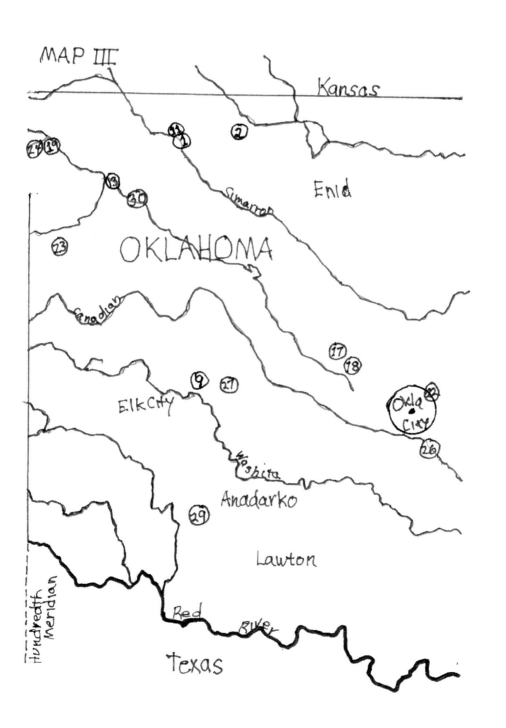

MAP III

Kansas

Enid

OKLAHOMA

Simarron

Canadian

Elk City

Washita

Anadarko

Lawton

Hundredth Meridian

Red River

Texas

Okla City

105

CPSIA information can be obtained at www.ICGtesting.com
Printed in the USA
BVOW07s0955040914

365383BV00001B/58/P